Cornelia J. M. Jordan

Flowers of Hope and Memory

a collection of poems

Cornelia J. M. Jordan

Flowers of Hope and Memory
a collection of poems

ISBN/EAN: 9783337090791

Printed in Europe, USA, Canada, Australia, Japan

Cover: Foto ©Andreas Hilbeck / pixelio.de

More available books at **www.hansebooks.com**

FLOWERS

OF

HOPE AND MEMORY:

A

Collection of Poems,

BY

CORNELIA J. M. JORDAN.

RICHMOND, VA.:
PUBLISHED BY A. MORRIS.
1861.

To

The Fireside and the Grave,

The Living and the Dead

of a

Broken Home-Circle,

This Volume is affectionately

and tearfully inscribed,

By

The Authoress.

CONTENTS.

CONTENTS.

PROEM.

WITH loving hands I humbly bring
  My little wreath of flowers;
Some gathered from the haunts of men,
  And some from wild wood bowers.

Some blossom'd in my life's glad Spring,
  Others in later years,
And some were cull'd and woven in
  The autumn time, of tears.

Some grew like sea-weeds, distant far,
  By sounding Ocean caves,
And some (dearest of all are these),
  Have blossom'd over graves.

No rare exotics mingle here
   Their rainbow hues combined,
But simple flowers alone look out
   And ask your welcome kind.

Such as they are,—for you, my friends,
   I've twined this wreath, to be
A votive offering at the shrine
   Of Hope and Memory.

FLOWERS OF HOPE AND MEMORY.

THE BRIDE OF HEAVEN.

She was arrayed as for a Bridal hour;
Round her fair forehead twined a matchless wreath
Of spotless Orange flowers, and her dark hair
Lay in rich, glossy folds, around a brow
Which wore the seal of youth and beauty too.
The smile of truth played on her coral lip,
And on her cheek the blush of innocence ;
While faith and hope beamed from her dark-brown
 eyes.
In the gay world I had known Genevieve,
A being loved and lovely. Yet I marked

That oft she seemed as some lone star, whose light
Waned in the skies, forsaken.   Oftentimes
A spell of brooding sadness darkly stole
Over her gentle spirit, causing friends
To marvel that her heritage of wealth,
And Nature's bounteous dower of rarest gifts,
Did fail to bring her happiness complete.
And there was one within whose noble heart
Her image lay, e'en like a mirror bright,
Which did reflect all that in Earth or Heaven
To him seemed beautiful.   Aye, and his love,
His first, fresh, early love was hers.   Alas!
That we should ever waste the treasured wealth
Of deep and true affection, on a heart
Within whose depths there ne'er can throb one pulse
Of answering sympathy.   She had long vowed
To let no human passion e'er find place
Within her maiden bosom, and the hour,
The solemn hour had come, when she should be
Declared the consecrated Bride of Heaven.
Lights shone resplendent through the vaulted dome
Of the old Convent Chapel; tapers bright

Gleamed softly through the aisles, and, here and
    there,
Lit up with mellow ray, the quaint Chef-d'œuvre
Of some old Master.

                Eager crowds pressèd in :
The young and old, the gay and sad of heart ;
Mirth with her jests, and Sorrow with her tears ;
Manhood and Beauty, Youth and Age were there.
And he was there, whose lofty brow was bent,
Whose heart was breaking at the sacrifice.
He saw the Orange wreath placed on her brow,
And in her hand, the mystic Crucifix,
While round her floated, gracefully, the veil.
Timidly, yet not with fear, she approached
The illumined altar, and the white-stoled Priest
Opened the Holy Book, and in loud voice ·
Asked the stern questions :

                " Dost thou here renounce
The world, its pomps and vanities ? Dost fling
Aside all ties of human love, and vow
To let no Earth-born passion e'er displace
The sacred love of Jesus ? Wilt forsake

All that the world holds dear, wealth, honors,
    friends,
To be henceforth the chosen bride of Christ ?"
A breathless silence reigned. The blushing cheek
Of the young novice paled, and gushing tears
Moistened her eyelids. Did a thought of home,
Of father, mother, and the parted band
Of brothers, sisters dear, wake in her heart
The slumbering chord of holiest affections?
Ah! did she feel in that stern, trying hour,
How hard it is, to coldly cast aside
Those who have loved us most; to sever ties
By God and Nature hallowed and blest? Did
Her cradle hymn, fresh from a mother's lip,
Chime with the Anthem; or the Organ's tone,
Wake the sweet memory of voices loved
In early childhood? Ah, could we've withdrawn
The secret veil which guarded thus, the heart
Of that fair girl, we might have witnessed there
The bitter struggle which her spirit felt
At yielding thus, the cherished ties of life.
One bright hope had armed her for the conflict,

And she must tear all others from her heart,
E'en though it break.   One gush of weeping more,
And she could then speak with unfaltering voice
The expected vow.
                Silence more silent grew,
Until the very air seemed hushed and still.
" Hearken," at length was said, in tones that drew
Their firmness from some superhuman source.
" Hearken, oh, Earth ! and Heaven give listening
      ear
To this, my utterance.   I do here renounce
Henceforth, forever, every mortal tie.
E'en from this hour, I take thee, Saviour mine,
To be my all in all.   For love of Thee
I do renounce all other loves.   Thy Cross
Shall be my talisman, and thy holy name
My chosen watchword.   That the world may know
I am no longer of it, this black veil
Shall soon displace the snowy one I wear.
Beneath its folds my consecrated face
Will be securely guarded from the view
Of men ; and, as a sacred sign, 'twill prove

That I can ne'er admit another love,
Than that I bear to Jesus."

     Hark, a sigh!
One deep-drawn sigh, and Rudolph looked his last
Upon his brave heart's idol. She withdrew
To veil her love-sealed features from man's gaze
Forever. * * * * * *
Quickly the scene was changed, and in her cell
Knelt Genevieve, a consecrated Nun,—
The sister Eulalie.

      No rich brocade
Now waved its silken folds about her form ;
No jewel sparkled from her close-veiled breast.
The coarse dark "habit" was her wedding dress,
A silver cross her bridal ornament.
Around her, freshly shorn from the young head,
Lay scattered strands of glossy, raven hair ;
And at her feet the snowy, orange wreath,—
An emblem meet of virgin purity.
O'er her fair brow the sombre "black veil" hung,
Shading, e'en like a cloud, her youthful face ;
And in low voice, she meekly counted o'er

The mystic beads, raising, anon, her eyes
To that bright Heaven, for which she had resigned
All, all the treasured hopes of earth.   She asked
That no regret might ever come to thwart
The solemn keeping of those holy vows,
Her lips had but just spoken.   As the prayer
Died on her virgin tongue, the Convent bell
Called her to matins ; and the saddened throng
Who came, as chosen witnesses, to see
Those solemn nuptial rites, heard the deep sound,
But as the death-knell of a cherished friend.
She only looked a hurried, last farewell,
And then withdrew, leaving a mournful spell
Of gloom upon us, as the massive door
Closed with an echo deep, upon those loved
Retiring footsteps we should hear no more.
A moment's pause, and clouds of incense rose,
Filling the air with fragrance.   Voices sweet
Chimed with the Organ's peal, and loudly, all
Proclaimed our Genevieve the Bride of Heaven.

THE PRAYER OF FAITH.

FATHER above!
Around whose throne the Cherubim are kneeling,
And Angels wait, their speechless praise revealing—
In whose pure presence veilèd Seraphs bend,
Awed by the light Thy dazzling glories lend,—
Hear, and remove
All blight of sin from out a heart defiled
By dross and stain of Earth—I am thy child.

Thou Light of Light!
Whose radiance fills the boundless sphere of Heaven,
Let one blest ray unto my soul be given,
And with its piercing radiance chase the gloom
Which hangs where Hope's fair blossoms fain would
bloom.
Cheer me to-night!

At Thy command sorrow and darkness flee !
Giver of Light, lift up my soul to thee.

Saviour divine !
On Calvary's mount Thy sacred heart was an-
    guished,
Thy body bruised, pierced, torn and bleeding, lan-
    guished ;
For us Thy brow, pressed by its thorny crown,
Pale with its "solemn agony," bowed down—
    Let Thy grace shine
In human hearts crushed now by mortal strife—
Send us Thy love to soothe, Giver of Life !

Spirit of Truth !
At thy behest the doubtful soul, and erring,
May lose its fears, Thy changeless law revering,
And resting all its wavering hopes on Thee,
Straight to the guidance of Thy wisdom flee—
    Bless Thou my youth !
Ere the "long night" cometh, seal with Thy love,
This heart I offer thee, Father above !

SONG OF THE MORNING SPRITE.

Lo! I come with a joyous step and free,
  The sunlight my brow adorning;
Dewy gems I wear in my shining hair,
  For I am the Sprite of Morning.

When I touch the Earth with my fairy wand,
  Lo! midnight and darkness vanish,—
The bright stars grow pale and the sweet moon-
    beams fail,
  As the Night's dull train I banish.

Hope, murmuring awhile in soft pensive tones,
  Her low sweet melodies humming,
Breaks out in wild song as I pass along,
  And cheerily greets my coming.

The flowers impatiently wait my smile,
  As, down in their green beds hidden,
They long for the day, as a child at play,
  Seeks a loving glance unbidden.

And I shake from their drowsy leaves dull sleep,
  I give to their bowed stalks lightness ;
I sprinkle the dew on their bosoms too,
  For they love its shining brightness.

The birds are all glad when my step draws near,
  As out, from their green boughs peeping,
Their warbles so clear, wake the zephyrs near,
  On the breasts of the flowers sleeping.

Heaven's glowing light is the crown I wear,
  No other my gay brow beareth ;
Its jewel, a Star, is more radiant far,
  Than gems the proud monarch weareth.

I laugh and I sport with all joyous things,
  I brighten the path of sadness ;

I know I am wild, but I'm Nature's child,
And mine is a life of gladness.

Lo! I come with a joyous step and free,
The sunlight my brow adorning;
Dewy gems I wear in my shining hair,
For I am the Sprite of Morning.

LITTLE THINGS.

LITTLE things—aye, little things,
   Make up the sum of life,—
A word, a look, a single tone,
   May lead to calm or strife.

A word may part the dearest friends—
   One, little, unkind word,
Which in some light, unguarded hour,
   The heart with anger stirred.

A look will sometimes send a pang
   Of anguish to the heart ;
A tone will often cause the tear
   In Sorrow's eye to start.

One little act of kindness done—
   One little soft word spoken,

Hath power to wake a thrill of joy,
    E'en in a heart that's broken.

Then let us watch these "*little things,*"
    And so respect each other,
That not a word, or look, or tone,
    May wound or vex a brother.

THOU ART GONE TO THE GRAVE.

THOU art gone to the grave, its cold portals closed
    o'er thee,
  While Hope's brilliant star o'er thy pathway did
    shine ;
  While Love's fairest flowers shed their fragrance
    around thee,
  And Youth's brightest treasures, sweet sister,
    were thine.

Thou art gone to the grave, its dark gloom is upon
    thee,
  And hushed is thy voice, full of kindness and
    love ;
Yet still in my happiest dreams I behold thee,
  All radiant with beauty and brightness above.

Thou art gone to the grave, with no stain on thy
    spirit,
  No shadow of sorrow or care on thy brow ;
All sinless and pure, endless bliss to inherit,
  In life's early morn thy dear form was laid low.

Thou art gone to the grave, yet ah, why should I
    mourn thee !
  Sweet flower, cut down in thy freshness and
    bloom.
Perhaps hadst thou lingered, misfortune had claimed
    thee,
  Or sorrow thrown o'er thee its withering gloom.

Thou art gone to the grave, and I would not recall
    thee,
  For all that the world gives of rapture or joy ;
Well I know that the kind arms of Jesus enfold
    thee,
  And pleasures unceasing thy moments employ.

THE MANSION BY THE SEA.

I KNOW a mansion, old and lone,
   Near by a Sea-girt shore—
Its ivied towers are crumbling piles,
   Its turrets grim and hoar,
And gaunt Decay in silence broods
Forever o'er its solitudes.

A lonely ruin, vast and grand,
   Mould on the sculptured walls,
While moth and lizard trail and creep
   Along the marbled halls.
There, when the Storm-king shows his face,
The Curlew finds a hiding-place.

No human forms are seen to glide
   This dreary Mansion near,

And through its aisles no voices ring
  In music wild and clear.
But day and night the Ocean surge
There echoes low, its plaintive dirge.

Once, near the spot, at sunset hour,
  An aged man I spied,
As, from the lonely, barren beach,
  I watched the foaming tide.
His form was bent, and from his brow
The Sea-breeze lifted locks of snow.

Long hours I marked him, silent, gaze
  Upon yon crumbling pile,
And down his furrowed cheek there rolled,
  A burning tear the while.
Ah! well I knew that Mansion dim
Waked mournful memories for him.

Perhaps 'twas here his boyhood passed;
  Perhaps a mother dear
First watched his timid, infant steps

And boyish beauty here.
Or, it may be, that here hath died
A gentle, loving, youthful Bride.

E'en as I mused, the Sun's last rays
    Lit up that ruin old,
Till all its towers were bathed in light,
    Its turrets crowned with gold.
And as the scene my thoughts beguiled,
The old man marked it too, and smiled.

Ere long his trembling steps approached,
    And, standing by my side,
He gazed, in silent awe, upon
    The darkly rolling tide.
And as a white Sail ploughed the main,
A tear-drop dimmed his eye again.

"They'll not come back to me, ah! no,"
    He turned, at length, and said,
" I'll not regain my treasures till
    The Sea gives up its Dead."

And to the calm, blue smiling sky,
He, upward, raised his tearful eye.

My questioning thoughts a look betrayed,
   And soon he thus began :
" Long, weary years have passed since *there*
   I lived a happy man."
And pointing to the Mansion old,
A tale of sorrowing love he told.

" 'Twas there I lived in calm content,
   For Heaven had smiled on me,
And loving eyes, with mine, looked out
   Upon the murmuring Sea.
But while I watched their tender light,
Death veiled them from my yearning sight.

" So perished from my side my wife,
   In youthful beauty's bloom,
And soon a smiling babe was laid
   Beside her in the tomb.
Yet though life's dearest joy was gone,
My stricken heart must still bear on.

" I felt that nought could fill again
 The void which Death had made,
Yet still around my lonely hearth,
 Two laughing children played.
These claimed my every thought and care,
My noble son and daughter fair.

" They grew to bless my fondest wish,
 And I, that they might be
Acquainted with my fatherland,
 Sent both across the Sea.
And from this spot I watched the tide
Which bore my children from my side."

He paused. " Where are they now ?" I asked.
 His answer was a sigh ;
And then he pointed to the Sea,
 And upward to the sky.
" An Ocean grave," I, musing, said ;
The old man bowed his hoary head.

The Sea-breeze sighed a requiem round
 That dim old Mansion grey,

As, o'er its towers and turrets now,
  The twilight shadows lay.
And as I turned to leave the strand,
The stranger seized my proffered hand.

"They came not back, in vain I watched
  Each coming sail in view;
The story of their fate, alas!
  No mortal ever knew.
No wreck was found—a fearful gale
Was all that told the sorrowing tale.

"My homestead yonder now became
  Intolerable to me,—
I could not bear a breeze or flower
  That whispered of the Sea.
Its doors were closed, and I became
A wanderer in heart and name.

         *   *   *   *   *   *

"But God is good, I know; and Heaven
  Not far away," he said.

" I shall regain my treasures when
   The Sea gives up its Dead."
And as I clasped his trembling hand,
Our tears fell mingling on the strand.

Long years have vanished since I heard
   That old man's parting sigh;
Yet never, while my heart can feel
   One sympathy, shall I
Forget the tale he told to me
Of that old Mansion by the Sea.

THE POOR.

Have pity on them, for their days
 Are cheerless, cold and drear;
And night, unwelcomed, comes to them
 With many a grief-born tear.
The scanty meal, the slender fire,
Tired Nature's unattained desire:
Alas! we know not half the care,
The poor, the very poor must bear.

Speak kindly to them, do not chide,—
 E'en though by sin and shame,
Their paths are darkened thus; yet oh!
 In pity do not blame.
His searching eye, who may endure,
To whom the purest are not pure,—

'Tis His alone to judge, not we,—
Poor heritors of misery.

Deal gently with them,—fearful Want
   Hath filled their hearts with pain ;
Perchance a word may wake the chords
   Of slumbering joy again.
Oh, to their gall-cup add not more :
Be kind, be soothing to the poor ;
For whatsoe'er their sins may be,
They still should claim our sympathy.

Give to them gladly, while thou hast,
   In mercy don't delay ;
When Fortune smiles, turn not thy face
   From helpless Want away.
Thy prompt assistance yet may save
Some brother from a hungered's grave ;
" Riches have wings;" ah ! wisely said,—
You too may beg your " daily bread."

DEATH OF THE HEART-FLOWER.*

'Twas a cheerless night—the last of Winter;
O'er the quiet town darkness now rested
Like a gloomy pall.   Not a sound was heard
Save when the restless winds swept howling by,
Eager for tempest.   In her lonely room
An anxious mother watched her suffering child;
And oh, how fraught with earnest love, and pain,
And silent anguish was that mother's vigil.
Close in its little cradle lay her charge,—
A babe of three bright summers.   On its cheek
Health glowed but yesterday, and feebly now
The crimson life-stream wanders through its veins.
Anxiously the skilled physicians watch, while
Gentle nurses wait around.

* On the death of Laura, infant daughter of Dr. William S. Morriss, of Lynchburg.

Slumber seals
The sufferer's eye, and hope springs up afresh
That morn will bring a change.   *   *   *
*   *   *   *   *   Fiercely without
The moaning wind sighs a last farewell to .
Winter. Through the distant sky, the threat'ning
Clouds roll on, and leave the pale, sweet moon
As clear, and calm, and bright, as if no hearts
Were breaking then beneath it.

Hark!
The old Church Clock strikes twelve. Winter has
     gone;
And up from Nature's bosom springs the breath
Of coming violets. O'er the Earth
A quiet stillness reigns—afar is heard
The music flow of waters, but the winds
Are hushed to silence, and the folded buds,
And birds, and flowers, wake on the breast of Spring.
A feeble moan calls the young mother now
Close to the cradle. Earnestly she bends
To catch some symptom of returning health;
But oh! the wish is vain. That brightening eye

Is but the spirit peering ere it takes
Its heavenward flight.
       The feeble pulse grows faint
And fainter, and around her neck are twined
The little arms that oft, in happier hours
Have fondled her before. "Too much, too much!"
Breaks from her lips in low convulsive sobs,
While friends, physicians, nurses, patient wait
For Death to claim his own.   Ah, how could *she*
Yield silently her treasure to his cold,
Freezing arms?   The heart so worn with watching
And with hope deferred, is breaking now; and,
Struggling with despair, at length pours forth
Its tide of pent-up anguish in one wild,
Piteous wail.
      "How can I give thee up,
Oh, child of many hopes and fondest love?
      Father, remove this cup
And send some other test my strength to prove.
      So lovely, gentle, mild,—
Laura, thy smiling beauty haunts me now,
      Sinless and undefiled!

Oh, must I see thy form in death laid low?
   Thy voice,—its music tone,
Rings through my ear in merry accents wild;
   How desolate and lone
Must be our hearth without thee, angel child?
   Stay, stay thy blow, stern Death!—
One moment let me gaze in that dear eye,
   And feel again the breath,
That fanned my throbbing breast in days gone by."

———Alas! too late.
   No smile of love, no look
Of recognition met her gaze. Feebly
The little arms slacken their hold. A sigh,
A restless stir, and then a quivering
Of the stricken frame, and all is over.
Her heart-flower had perished with the morning
  dawn
Of Spring.

EULALIE.

EULALIE, when first I saw thee,
   Thy young heart was blithe and free,
And the charm of youthful beauty,
   Threw its radiance over thee.
Thou wert in the Convent Garden;
   I recall the moment well;
'Twas when o'er the fragrant blossoms,
   Twilight's dewy shadows fell.
By thy side, were Nuns repeating
   Vespers to the Virgin mild:
" Holy mother, guard, protect her,
   Save from sin our Novice child."
And I gazed on thee and wondered
   If thy heart knew nought of care,
And if blighted human passion
   Left no farewell shadow there.

Then I watched a bright smile playing
  In thy beaming eye again,
And I felt that life had spared thee,
  All its bitterness and pain.
Thou wert like a wild flower growing
  On some lonely river's brink,—
Waiting only for the tempest
  In its silent waves to sink.
Months rolled on, I learned to love thee,
  With devoted, earnest love;
Thou wert all my dreams had pictured
  Of the "pure in heart" above.
I have sat for hours and listened
  To the music of thy voice;
And thy very name, thy footstep,
  Made my youthful heart rejoice.
Oft I'd paint the distant future,—
  Thou wert e'er its day-star bright;
And thy cherished form was near me,
  In each holy dream at night.
Till at length life's early sorrow,
  In my spirit's depth found place,

When I saw the sombre "black veil"
   Shade thy young and happy face.
And I heard thy own lips utter,
   In their low, sweet music tone :
" Hearken, friends, henceforth I sever
   Human ties for God alone."
Then they threw a black pall o'er thee :
   " To the world thou'rt dead," they said ;
And they clipped the raven tresses,
   From thy meekly-bending head.

   *   *   *   *   *   *

Eulalie, we now are parted—
   I am still thy faithful friend ;
We are parted, yet affection
   With my life alone can end.
I recall with fond emotion
   Every stern and holy truth,
Which thy lips have ever taught me,
   Gentle Guardian of my youth.
And I ponder oft the lessons
   That I used to learn of thee ;

Whilst methinks I hear thee utter,

   With a blessing, prayers for me.

But our lots are cast asunder,

   And our paths are severed wide;

Thy duties shun the world's rough Sea, ·

   Mine bear me with the tide.

Yet though perhaps on earth again

   Thy face I ne'er may see,

My soul, through life, will fondly nurse

   Thy memory, Eulalie.

TO SPRING.

ONCE more we gladly greet thee, joyous Spring—
   Clothed in thy dew-gemmed robe of rainbow dye;
The smiling Earth, the flowing streams, the flowers,
   All welcome with delight thy genial sky.

And we, who've sighed for Summer sunshine long—
   We too unite with bird, and brook, and bee,
To hail the music whispers of the winds—
   Glad Nature's melodies that tell of thee.

Long have we shivered 'neath the Snow-king's
      breath,
   And mourned the blight of dreary Winter's reign;
Now warmed to light by thy soft, winsome touch—
   The violets leave their frozen beds again.

And ice-bound rivulets flow, sparkling on
    Through flowery meadows bathed in dewy light;
And birds are busy in the forest bowers—
    Wooing lost mates to join their airy flight.

Already flies the summer Oriole near,
    Seeking the sheltering bough, from which to swing
The oval nest, wherein, secure, her young
    May bide all storm, hid 'neath her cosy wing.

And, here and there, in sunny places gleam
    The sweet Forget-Me-Nots from mossy dells;
While golden Buttercups their welcomes breathe
    By lifting to thy glance their dewy bells.

What glories waken as thy steps draw near,
    What joy thou bearest on thy gladsome wing;
Hope blooms afresh, health follows in thy train—
    A radiance lights thy shining pathway, Spring!

Then once again we gladly greet thy smile,
    Bathing in rosy light the dewy morn;
On human hearts by Sorrow's winter seared,
    Thou shedd'st, of prayerful hope, a brightening
        dawn.

A DIRGE FOR LAURA.

Lay her beneath the willow,
Let soft violets be her pillow;
Far, far from the Ocean billow
   Let the young and lovely rest.

Cover her grave with flowers;
And in Summer's golden hours
Let the gentle evening showers
   Fall above her silent breast.

Be not sad or broken-hearted,
That the loved one hath departed,
For no cloud of sin e'er darted
   Thwart her life's unsullied sky.

Therefore cease, fond mother, cease your weeping,
Her pure soul is in God's keeping;
And her little form is sleeping
    In the still earth peacefully.

THE FLOWERS HAVE COME.

THE flowers have come—from its mossy bed
The Violet lifts up its modest head ;
The Daisy, too—poor shy little thing,
Has opened its bright eyes to welcome the Spring.

The flowers have come—for the soft perfume
Of the Wallflower sweet, and the Rose's bloom
Is borne on the wing of the mild South breeze,
As it lovingly plays through the leafy trees.

The flowers have come—near the garden walk
The proud Lily raises its queenly stalk ;
The Buttercup opens its golden bell,
To take in the sunbeams it loves so well.

The flowers have come—see, the red Woodbine
Wreathes its verdant leaves with the Jessamine vine ;

The Humming-bird, lured by the sweet perfume,
Sips joy all day from its honeyed bloom.

The flowers have come—I have seen the Bee
Now kiss the bright clover that blooms in the lea,
Then buzzing away, like a heartless coquette,
Woo the very next innocent blossom he met.

The flowers have come—on the river's brink
The Daffodils cunningly nod and wink
To the ripples that sportively trifle all day,
With the blossoms that spring in their pebbly way.

The flowers have come—lo! the Crocus too,
With its leaves of purple, and white, and blue,
Looks up from its home with the Cowslip sweet,
The smile of its mother, the Spring, to greet.

The flowers have come—even now I feel
Their fragrant breath o'er my senses steal;
Lifting my heart, in its happiest hours,
To Him who has brightened life's path with flowers.

LINES

ON THE DEATH OF MRS G. S. MEEM.

"Oh! for the world where thy home is now.
How may we love—but in doubt and fear,
How may we anchor our fond hearts here.
How should e'en joy, but a trembler be,
Beautiful dust, when we look on thee!"

HEMANS.

Ah, brief indeed was life's fair dream,
Sweet Friend, to thee!
How "passing strange" and sad doth seem
Thy destiny.

Two fleeting months—and thou didst stand,
A timid Bride;
And he who claimed thy "heart and hand,"
Stood by thy side.

5*

With rapt'rous ear he heard thee breathe
    Love's fervent vow,
And saw the Orange blossoms wreathe
    Thy queenly brow.

What blissful joy then did light
    His loving eye.
Ah! little thought he, one so bright
    Could surely die.

Too true, alas! the grave's cold breath
    Is on thee now;
No more the beauteous "bridal wreath"
    Bedecks thy brow.

Fond hearts that loved thee, now are sad,
    And sigh in vain;
For thy dear smile to cheer and glad
    Their home again.

They who around thy couch of pain
    Did watch and weep,

Mourn now, that nought shall break again
    Thy dreamless sleep.

She too, who soothed with gentle hand
    Thy burning brow,
Sees now the fairest of her band
    In death laid low.

Ah, little reck'st thou of the tears
    Thus vainly shed ;
For hushed are all thy trembling fears,
    Thou sinless dead.

Blest, happy spirit—thou dost roam
    In realms of light ;
And to thy distant, radiant home,
    Shall come no blight.

No withering flowers there shall bind
    Thy gentle brow :
A fadeless wreath, by Angels twined,
    Adorns thee now.

The joys that crown that life above,
　　Ah, who can tell!—
He calls thee hence whose name is Love,—
　　Dear one—farewell!

THE SUMMER RAIN.

WAKING gales that slumbered long
  In the woodland bowers,
Flinging odors on the air
  · From a thousand flowers;
Knocking with a gentle tap
  'Gainst my window pane,
'Mid the sultry glare of noon,
  Comes the Summer Rain.

Glittering showers from rainbow skies,
  Sparkling drops so bright,
Coming with a pattering step,
  Fill us with delight;
Little flowerets, drooping long,
  Lift their heads again;

Little rills with merry song,
　　Hail the Summer Rain.

Bird and bee with folded wing
　　Watch the cooling showers,
From their hiding-places sweet,
　　'Mong the smiling flowers;
Nature's welcome-chorus glad,
　　Echoes o'er the plain;
Blooming fields of waving corn
　　Laugh and sing again.

From the ground a thousand sweets
　　Gratefully arise,
Through the air a perfumed breath
　　Wafting to the skies;
Flocks and herds delighted stand,
　　Verdure decks the plain;
Earth, rejoicing, claps her hands,—
　　Lo! the Summer Rain.

THERE'S A CLOUD ON MY SPIRIT.

There's a cloud on my spirit,
  A gloom in my heart;
A shadow, a something,
  That will not depart.
I've struggled in vain, love!
  To drive off the spell,
Which fain the heart's music
  With murmurs would quell.
I've gazed from my window,
  This beautiful day,
And clouds dim the landscape,
  Before me alway.
I know 'tis not Autumn,
  E'en now in the bowers,
I hear the birds singing
  Of Spring to the flowers.

The clover is nodding
   Its head to the bee,
As zephyrs approach it,
   Far off in the lea.
The sunlight is gleaming
   Through green forest woods,
Yet darkening the picture
   A dim shadow broods.
All glad things are around me,
   And whispering nigh;
Yet, yet I am lonely,
   And cannot tell why.
What is it that hides thus
   The sunshine of life,
And stills the heart's music
   With melody rife?
It cannot be Winter,
   For now in the bowers,
The birds are all singing
   Of Spring to the flowers.
I'll ask them the secret,
   Perhaps they can tell,

Why broods o'er my spirit
   This shadowy spell?
The question propounded,
   They laugh at me, dear;
While my heart gives the answer
   That *you are not here!*

G

MUSINGS AT THE GRAVE OF A YOUNG SISTER.*

BENEATH this sod thou'rt lowly laid, oh, cherished
    one and dear—
Thou, at whose name Affection gives to Memory's
    claim—a tear.
Long years, long, weary years have passed, since
    last we looked on thee,
And yet to-day blooms fresh as then, thy fadeless
    memory.
The lonely void which thou hast left, no other form
    may fill,
Within our hearts, as in our home, thy place is
    sacred still.
I look around,—but yesterday it seems, since glad
    and gay,

* Who died, a school-girl, at the Academy of the Visitation,
Georgetown, D. C., Sept. 9th, 1846.

Thy smile shone brightest in our midst,—a sun-
　　beam in our way.
Oh, when life's pathway seemed so bright—Hope's
　　prophesy so fair,
Why did Death shade thy gentle brow,—why place
　　his signet there?
And while Affection's glowing font so fondly gushed
　　for thee,
Why did'st thou leave us, birdling bright, away
　　from earth to flee?
Far, far in childhood's sunny home, were loving
　　hearts that yearned
To clasp thee, darling, but to them thy step no more
　　returned.
I saw the rose fade from thy cheek, sweet, laughter-
　　loving child,—
For months I watched thy drooping eye,—its
　　brightness strange and wild.
And sometimes there would come the thought (but
　　oh, how could it be
Long harbored in a breast so full of earnest love
　　and thee?)

That thou wert fading, day by day—Disease with
blighting breath,—

A withering simoon, bowing thee to an untimely
death.

Then all thy blooming loveliness, thy beauty's
matchless spell,

Would drive from my too blinded heart the fears
I dared not tell.

And though the "hectic" on thy cheek, its paleness seemed to share,

I dreamed not Death's cold dart would aim at one
so strangely fair.

At length upon a couch of pain, I watched thee
patient wait

The message that must summon thee beyond the
eternal gate.

No dark despair, no doubt, no fear, thy peaceful
bosom stirred,—

"I've left my home to die," was said without one
murmuring word.

An Angel's arms were round thee then,—I knew
it by the smile

Of heavenly hope that beamed upon thy suffering
    face the while.
Yes, holy angels waited near, impatiently, to bear
Thy soul to that far, radiant land, where endless
    pleasures are.
I knew that thou wert dying, yet alas! I could not
    save,
E'en by my heart's deep anguish, our bright Star-
    ling from the grave.
But ah! since to the "pure in heart" Death brings
    no bitter sting,
Why shouldst thou fear to sleep beneath the Ever-
    lasting wing.
One look, one farewell glance on us, who wept
    around thy bed,
And then, on viewless pinions borne, thy gentle
    spirit fled.

   *   *   *   *   *   *   *   *

I saw the form I fondly loved wrapped in the
    " winding sheet ;"
I called,—those lips would part no more, Affec-
    tion's voice to greet.

They laid thee in thy girlhood's bloom, our young-
    est, fairest, best,
With all thy maiden loveliness, low, in the grave's
    cold breast.
That mournful scene, oh, Memory, hide, I dare not
    dwell too long,—
It wakes within my heart a chord of anguish wild
    and strong.
Methinks I see thee, sister mine, as then, a lifeless
    mould,
Thy wasted hands crossed on thy breast,—thy
    forehead pale and cold.
But ah, a brighter vision dawns, by Faith in mercy
    given ;
I gaze, and lo! thou com'st to me, an angel bright
    from Heaven !
I know thy sinless soul is free, and ne'er again
    shall pine,
Yet oh, forget not those whose hearts in life were
    linked with thine.
Still hover near his bending form, and soothe his
    grief-worn brow,

Whose father-love through long, long years, doth
    claim remembrance now ;
And we, the still remaining two, who miss thee from
    our side,
Whenever morning's splendor shines, or evening's
    shadows glide.
Remember us in that bright land where sainted
    spirits stray,
And to those blissful realms above, oh, gently
    point the way.
Be near, our guardian angel still, when luring
    snares beguile,
In health and sickness, life and death, be near us
    all the while.
And when at last we, too, shall sleep within the
    grave's dark breast,
Oh, may our souls like thine awake in realms of
    endless rest.
Now, fare thee well ; thy cherished form lies cold
    beneath this sod,
Yet well I know thy spirit pure rejoices with its
    God.

INVOCATION.

TELL me, ye Stars of night,
Is there beyond your burning orbs of light
    A home—a heaven ;
Where spirits of the just, the pure, the blest,
Are sheltered from all storms in realms of rest,
    Where peace is given ?

To that far world of bliss,
That realm of light, can all the woes of this
    No shadows bring ?
Flows there a Lethean stream whose silent wave
Once sipped by the departed, e'er will save
    From Memory's sting ?

Do flowers ne'er fade and die
In that bright land, and in each pathway lie,
    Stripped of their bloom ?

Comes there no Autumn, with its chilling breath,
To stamp them with the livid hues of death—
    No Winter's gloom?

Do angels, too, dwell there,
And tones of seraph voices fill the air
    With music sweet?
And do the saints, God's faithful children here,
Rest from their toils in that heavenly sphere—
    Their joy complete?

'Mid that celestial host
May they be found, the loved and early lost,
    Whom we've mourned so long;
And at the evening hour when smiles and mirth
Have met in gladness round the social hearth
    Missed from our throng?

Are there no farewells spoken,
No bright eyes dimmed with tears, no fond heart
    broken
    On that blest shore?

But do the severed links of Friendship's chain
Meet there in gladness and unite again
    Bright as before ?

Oh, give me Faith's glad wings,
That I may soar above terrestrial things,
    To realms on high ;
Where they have gone whom I have loved so well,
And where, when life is o'er, I too, may dwell
    Eternally.

TO LITTLE EMILY.

God's blessing on thee, darling,
  Through thy life, as it rests now,
In the heavenly expression
  Of thy little baby brow.

What a world of teeming glories
  Now has burst upon thy sight,
With its thousand varied beauties,
  And its fields all bathed in light.

How I love to watch thy features
  As thy brightly beaming eye
Gazes up, as if in wonder,
  At the splendor of the sky.

Ay, and then, as though applauding
   All thy Maker's skill the while,
Soon I see the sweet lips parting
   In a merry baby smile.

Listen, hark!—why start enchanted?
   It was but a joyous bird,
Whose gay song among the leafy trees
   In gladsome notes you heard.

Look, see there!—on lightning pinion
   He is darting through the air;
Ah, how bright his warbling spirit
   And his downy feathers are.

What are all thy thoughts, my darling,
   Of this lovely world of ours,—
Seems it bright to thy young spirit,
   Newly strayed from Eden bowers?

Yes, I know it by the gladness,
   To thy heart and features given,

That a something lingers round thee
    Of the radiance of Heaven.

Oh, may future years bring to thee
    Nought to mar thy soul's delight; ·
May Time hold for thee, fair cherub,
    No dark, distant, coming blight.

But be all thy life as joyous
    As the gushing song of bird,
And thy spirit's wave be never
    By Sin's dark'ning ripples stirred.

That when Death draws near to claim thee,
    He may wear an Angel's face,
And the grave, to thee, be only
    But a blessed resting-place.

A FAREWELL TO THE DYING YEAR.

Good-bye, Old Year! I take thy hand in sadness,
  And gaze all tearfully along the Past,—
When I did welcome thee with smiles and gladness,
  And golden hopes too wildly dear to last;
When, through Time's mystic veil, in wisdom
    shading
  The unseen Future's dim uncertain maze,
With Youth's bright prophet-dreams my vision
    lading,
  I strove, in restless eagerness, to gaze.

And as I caught that future's faint revealing,
  Breaking upon my heart with shadowy spell;
And felt the gloom of disappointment stealing
  O'er dreams my foolish heart had nursed too well;

Ah, then I marvelled that Earth's transient glories
  Could thus allure the soul's immortal trust;
And I did learn that Pleasure's siren stories
  Are gilded legends gathered from the dust.

Yet I've no harsh reproach, no vain complaining
  To weave with this, my parting lay to thee,
For thou hast mingled joys, bright and unfeigning,
  In every cup thy hand hath proffered me;
And though, at times, the "bitter" I have tasted,
  Till all my soul seemed poisoned by its gall,
Yet I have felt these lessons were not wasted—
  Some prayer, unsaid before, hath followed all.

And now I kneel, to bless, not to upbraid thee,
  That thou hast wisely scattered thorns with
    flowers;
Since, varying thus my pathway, thou hast made me
  Look upward yearningly to Heaven's changeless
    bowers.
There, Joy's ecstatic season is not measured
  By Time's swift-failing sands so quickly run;

But, in Eternity's deep bosom treasured,
　　Our days, and months, and moments, all are one.

And I would thank thee too, with fond emotion,
　　That from her grave, whose eyes thy hand did'st
　　　close,
There comes to me a voice of sweet devotion,
　　For faith which placed on Heaven its high re-
　　　pose—
That thus I learn, from lips now sealed forever,
　　Whose prayerful tones fell on my childhood's ear,
That all in vain my spirit's wild endeavor
　　For lasting joy, while darkly wandering here.

And for those household bands thou leavest un-
　　broken,
　　In their deep, tender sympathies, how dear,—
That, kindly yet the mandate is unspoken,
　　Which bids them part, I bless thee, Dying Year.
Now, with full heart, my inmost bosom swelling,
　　And holy thoughts I may not pause to tell,
And gushing tears from Memory's fountain welling,
　　I breathe again, Old Year, my last farewell.

TO A CROSS.

"In hoc signo spes mea."

EMBLEM of love divine!
Thou speak'st to me of Calvary's holy hill,
Where Jesus, bowing to his Father's will,
Yielded his life for mine.

What pain, what agony,
O'erwhelmed his spirit in that fearful hour,
When love, subduing every sterner power,
Bled for humanity.

Nature's offended eye
Would not behold him of each friend bereft,
And on that drear and lonely mountain left
To suffer, groan, and die.

The Temple's veil was rent,
The glorious Sun withdrew his cheering light,
And earth was sunk in universal night,—
Man lost in wonderment.

One true heart scorned him not ;
When in all other bosoms pity slept,
Mary, his mother, sat her down and wept
O'er his forsaken lot.

So may I, Saviour, cling
In every trial to thy bleeding side,
And in thy wounds my weeping spirit hide
From stern Despair's dark sting.

Teach me this truth profound,
And let my heart the useful lesson know,
That in this dim and tearful vale below,
Happiness is not found.

But by thy Cross and love,
Oh! may I learn to purify from sin
Each inward feeling, that my soul may win
A crown of bliss above.

THE MANIAC GIRL.

(FROM A SCENE IN A LUNATIC ASYLUM.)

SHE wept in anguish, clasped her hands, and madly
    tore her hair,
And thus, in accents strange and wild, she raved
    in her despair :
" Oh God ! remove this iron weight that hangs
    about my heart,
Speak, Thou Almighty, speak, and bid this raven
    form depart.
I cannot live,—yet dare not die by my own feeble
    hand :
Against the act Thy word hath fixed a fearful,
    dark command.
I dare not take what Thou hast given, and yet, my
    God, I crave
The unbroken peace, the silence deep, the oblivion
    of the grave.

The grave—oblivion—ha! ha! ha!—a wiser one
    hath said

Dark dreams may come, there may not be oblivion
    for the dead.

If so, and I should sip to-day a draught of Death's
    cold wine,

What dreams of dark and dread despair, what
    visions would be mine!

These crushing memories, would they come to
    haunt me in the grave?

My broken hopes—*his trifling!* Oh! one draught
    from Lethe's wave."

*   *   *   *   *   *   *   *

"It may not be; I must bear on, despite this anguish
    wild.

Father, then hear with pitying ear, the heart's
    prayer of Thy child.

Take from me every murmuring thought, and, if it
    be Thy will

To chasten thus, then let these ghastly phantoms
    haunt me still.

It may be, when all others fail, I'll learn to lean on
    Thee,

Since Thou alone canst fill the heart, who fill'st
    immensity !
Thou, only Thou, canst say to grief's wild passion-
    storm, ' Be still !'
And Thou alone canst soothe the spirit's anguish
    at Thy will.
Hear me, Oh ! God, my Father ! take this weight
    from off my heart,
Or bid all restless, murmuring thoughts forever to
    depart."

    *   *   *   *   *   *   *   *

The prayer went up through Mercy's gate, low
    bows the youthful head,—
A calm smile lights the pale, sweet face—the maniac
    girl is dead.

TO A MINIATURE OF THE DEAD.

YES, sister dear, this is thine image own;
This glad smile thy joyous heart's expression.
Fondly I love to gaze, e'en though through tears,
Upon each feature, and in each to trace
The sinless beauty of an Angel face.
And can it be, beloved, that thou art dead?
That on that brow, so pure and beautiful,
Death's seal is resting now? that those soft eyes
No more will open on Life's glorious things?
Those laughing lips ne'er part to speak to me?
Oh! sister mine, tell me what radiant sphere
Contains thy spirit? In its holy clime,
Dost thou retain aught of the love of earth?
Am I now less thine own, because I tread
These darkened pathways still, which thou hast left?
Or dost thou backward gaze o'er life's dim track,

And, mid the glories of that brighter world,
Pity the woes of this?

       Ah, well I know
That in the mansions of the "pure in heart"
Thou hast a place; and when I look around
On all the evil which surrounds us here,
I thank my God that thou, so long, sweet dove,
Hast folded thy glad wings in Paradise.

HARSH WORDS.

AIR—"*Kind words can never die.*"

HARSH words can never die;
  Deeply they rest,
In all their rankling power,
  Down in the breast.
What though one may forgive,
  And all regret be met
With kind response?   Alas!
  None can forget.

Harsh words will darkly rise
  In happiest hours,
Rank thorns in Memory's path,
  Crushing the flowers;
Rank weeds, whose poisonous breath
  Mildew and blight unfold,

Wasting the heart like Death,
  Chilling and cold.

Harsh words, once spoken, stand,—
  Tear drops that fall
On Ocean's rolling waves,
  Who can recall?
So by unkindness moved,
  Deeply the heart must feel
Wounds, which, though pardoned all,
  Nothing can heal.

Oh then beware, beware!
  Weigh well each word,
Lest in some tender breast
  Anguish be stirred;
Lest when 'tis all too late,
  Thou wouldst call back again
Harsh words, whose memory
  Mocks thee in vain.

8

A MEMORY.

'Twas on a balmy morning in the month of May,
When the busy song of birds, and scent of flowers
Bespoke the glad return of Spring.

                        I stood
Beside a couch, where lay the pale death-stricken
    form
Of a fair girl. The fresh breeze as it murmured by,
Soft fanned the glossy ringlets of her dark-brown
    hair,
And cooled the fevered throbbing of her snow-white
    brow.
She *had* been beautiful, and even now disease
Had scarcely robbed her of her youth's bright
    bloom; yet sure
Consumption with its blighting breath wasted her
    frame,

And stole the gentle rose-hue from her maiden
    cheek,
Leaving the brilliant "hectic" in its place. She
    lay
The uncomplaining victim to an early doom.
And softly by her side, in low convulsive sobs,
(Lest troubled grief like hers disturb the flowing
    fount
Of deep, strong, deathless love within the sufferer's
    heart),
Her mother wept.
                And seeing that a fevered sleep ·
Half sealed her dear one's eye, she in her wild
    despair
Believed her dying. Raising her sad eyes to
    Heaven,
As if to implore, in prayer, that God would kindly
    will
" The bitter cup to pass," she exclaimed in anguish :

" Oh my child ! my child ! I cannot see thee die,
Nor watch the fading brightness of thine eye.

Thou art my widowed heart's idolatry,—
   I cannot see thee die !
How I should miss thy gentle voice's tone,
Thou, my first born, my beautiful, my own;
Oh ! I could ne'er tread Earth's bleak path alone,
   When thou, my child, art gone !"

 * * * * * * * *

   Starting, as if some thrilling dream
Had broken her peaceful slumber, her pale, wasted
  face
Radiant with a smile of sweet tranquillity,—
The maiden woke, and opening her large, languid
  eyes,
Fixed them upon her mother, and began :

" Mother, draw near, I must leave thee now :
The cold dews of Death are upon my brow.
I must quit thy embrace and the home of my love;
But I go to a far brighter dwelling above.
I'll twine a bright chaplet of fair flowers there,
For thee,—meet reward for thy fond, gentle care,—

And o'er thee a spirit's kind vigil I'll keep.
Oh mother, sweet mother, I pray do not weep.
Ne'er again shall I know either sickness or care :
Disease, Death, nor sorrow can e'er reach me there.
Mother ! the harp-notes of angels I hear,—
They're wooing my soul to that heavenly sphere.
I go—fare thee well"—

But the next word was spoken in Heaven,
For her pure soul had gone back to its God, and
    now
The afflicted mother, bowing her chastened heart
In meek submission to Heaven's stern decree,
Murmured, " Thy will be done !"

A LITTLE CHILD'S PRAYER.

Low I bend my knee before Thee,
　Gracious Saviour, meek and mild;
Hear the prayer my young lips utter,
　Thou wert once, like me,—a child.

In this world, a trembling stranger,
　Timidly I grope alway,
For I know that foes are lurking
　To entice my steps astray.

Let Thy gracious hand then guide me
　O'er life's dark and troubled tide,—
Take me under Thy protection,
　Keep me ever near Thy side.

Let my footsteps never wander
  From thy paths thou guid'st me in ;
Screen, Oh ! Lord, my soul from danger,
  Guard my helpless heart from sin.

And when Death shall come to bear me
  From the scenes of Earth away,
May my spirit find its guerdon,
  In the realms of endless day.

There to join the praise eternal
  Of the myriad Angel host,
Who surround Thy throne, adoring
  Father, Son, and Holy Ghost.

"I WOULD NOT LIVE ALWAYS."

I WOULD not live always, though fortune should
  smile,
And pleasure should gladden my path all the while;
Though friends should surround me to comfort and
  cheer,
I still would not linger eternally here.

I would not live always, though glory and fame,
Should follow my footsteps and honor my name;
Though joy like a sunbeam should brighten my way,
And peace in my heart shed its shadowless ray.

I would not live always, when they I most love
Have gone from this earth to their blest homes
  above.

When the fond ties that bind us to life are all riven,
Oh, who would then linger an alien from Heaven!

I would not live always, when Death can restore
The friends I have loved and give back as before
Each link that hath dropped from Affection's bright
  chain,
And bind us in Love's golden bondage again.

I would not live always—no, fain would I fly
To that bright land of promise beyond the blue sky,
Where the sad work of sorrow forever is o'er,
And partings and farewells are heard of no more.

TO A FRIEND.

FOR A BOUQUET DURING ILLNESS.

THANKS, many thanks, for your lovely flowers;
They have sweetly gladdened my weary hours,—
They bring a smile in the sad heart to glow,
And a perfumed breath for the fevered brow.
Flowers! they wake in the Invalid's breast
Glad thoughts of Earth in her Spring beauty drest;
Of the open field and the forest wild,—
Where Nature's own glory hath brightly smiled.
I pine for the cool mountain's shady stream,
Where the bright-eyed blossoms in beauty gleam
From the sloping bank, and then stooping lave
Their light, pearly cups in the sparkling wave.
What would the Spring be, though a vocal train
Of forest warblers still herald her reign,

If no blushing buds in our pathway grew,
Or lilies to gather the soft May dew?
And what of the honey bee,—can ye tell
Where his light, airy form all day would dwell
In the Summer hours, if no sweet-celled bloom
Allured him not with its honeyed perfume?
Flowers! they are gems on the breast of Earth;
How holy their mission, how pure their worth!
Oh! for that clime where no chill, autumn blight,
Can wither their freshness, or fade their light.
Thanks, gentle friend, for your sweet gift to me;
It wakens a wish in my heart for thee,
That ever through life from Love's roseate bowers
Your hand may gather the choicest flowers.

SHADOWS OF MEMORY.

ONE moment to my throbbing heart I clasped thee,
    darling boy,—
One moment felt the gushing of a mother's holy joy.
And while I gazed with rapture on thy matchless
    infant charms,
Death's envious Angel softly came, and stole thee
    from my arms.
And oh, so stealthily he crept—so gently hushed
    thy breath,
It seemed almost a mockery, to say that such was
    Death.
So full of love and hope was I, that blessèd April
    morn,
I scarce had felt thou wert my own, my beautiful
    first-born.

And e'en while I implored for strength, my babe,
    that I might be
Thy only mother,—that no stranger breast might
    nurture thee,
They took thee sleeping from my side, and laid
    thee snug and low—
Close by, within thy cradle-bed, as soft and white
    as snow.
And there, in holy slumber wrapt, I watched thee
    all the while,
Until my mother-fondness grew impatient for thy
    smile ;
I longed to see thee ope thine eye, but wished alas,
    in vain—
How little dreaming then that thou wouldst never
    wake again.
At length so breathless still thy sleep, so motion-
    less thy head,
That earnestly I begged they would just lay thee
    on my bed ;
Where I might note each restless stir, and catch
    each half-drawn sigh,

And if a sound disturbed, speak one soft word of
"lullaby."

But no; "So sweet he rests," they said, "he must
not wakened be,"

And I, thus feeble, must not feel too anxious, love,
for thee.

They *meant* it kind, but I have felt, sometimes, in
my despair,

That, had they brought thee to *my* arms, I might
have *kept* thee there;—

So closely nestled to my heart, my birdling might
have been

Warmed into life, if love could win the spirit back
again.

The weary hours dragged slowly on, till others
feared, like me,

That thy long slumber was too deep, and softly
crept to see.

All mutely gazed!—I watched each mien—thy
little helpless head

Hung still and cold upon thy breast,—oh, God!
my child was dead.

* * * * * * * *

Yes, in the morning of thy life, ere sin could mar
    thy day,
A band of smiling Cherubs came, and wooed thy
    soul away.
Soft Angel-voices in thy sleep told thee, in whispers
    low,
Of deathless flowers in Paradise, and bade thee,
    darling, go.
If thou hadst only known the love that wildly
    gushed for thee,
Ah, then I might have borne to let my little pet
    dove flee.
Or if thou erst had parted that sweet coral mouth
    of thine
To lisp but one soft word of love, in answer back
    to mine,
I might have felt to see thee die, thou couldst not
    then forget
Thy mother's wild idolatry, which lingers, baby,
    yet.
But ah, to yield thee thus, my boy—to give thee up
    to Death,

Ere I had scarcely felt the glow of thy soft per-
    fumed breath!
'Tis this that mocks my agony! Yet I will not
    despair,
Since Heaven is thine, and I may still clasp thee,
    my lost one, there.
Oh, from that far off spirit land, where all is joy
    divine,—
Where thou, mid radiant Seraph hosts, the loveliest
    far, doth shine,
Sweet baby, sometimes give one thought—one kindly
    thought to me,
And let thy mother feel that she is not estranged
    from thee.
Hear this fond prayer, in anguish breathed,—and
    on thy glad wing flee,
And bear it to His throne, who ne'er couldst turn
    away from thee.
That where my child, my Angel-child, and little
    Willie are,
I too may go, when life is o'er,—and *thou mayst
    know me there.*

WHAT A ZEPHYR TOLD ME.

I'M a beautiful zephyr,
　　Light, airy, and free;
And I roam the wide world,
　　O'er the Land and the Sea.
I follow old Winter
　　With warmth on my wing;
And the Poets have called me
　　The breathing of Spring.
I kiss the young flowers,
　　And they wake to the light;
At my voice the birds carol
　　Their songs of delight.
I climb the tall mountain,
　　I rove through the plain,

9*

And I sport with the billows
   On Ocean's broad main.
I fan the sweet garden-beds
   With my soft wing,
And lo! from their dewy breasts
   Violets spring.
The rivulets owe all
   Their music to me,
For I conquer the Ice-King
   And thus, they are free.
I fan the poor Invalid's
   Brow, and its gloom
Fades in light, 'neath the breath
   Of my rosy perfume.
I lure the dull honey-bee
   Back to the flowers,
And I wake the winged warblers
   In green forest bowers.
I'm a beautiful zephyr,
   Light, airy, and free;
And I roam the wide world,
   O'er the Land and the Sea.

I follow old Winter
  With warmth on my wing;
And the Poets have called me
  The breathing of Spring.

LITTLE CARLTON.

A LAMENT.*

He came to us—a thing of joy,
  Filling our home with glee;
No warbling bird upon the wing
  Seemed half so blithe as he.

The face so bright, e'er sickness dimmed
  The light within his eyes;
The tottering step, the laughing shout,
  The look of glad surprise—

All now are sad remembered things,
  That come to mock despair;
And yet our fond hearts love to hold
  Each treasured picture fair.

---

* Inscribed to his father and mother,—Mr. and Mrs. John R. Steptoe, of Virginia.

For while we watched his angel smile,
    Heaven seemed not far away—
We dreamed not that a phantom-form
    Followed him, day by day.

But oh, at length the Spoiler drew
    Nearer, with stealthy tread,
And marked the prize—our darling bowed
    His little, sinless head.

For months, with anxious, prayerful hearts,
    We watched him day by day,
As with hushed song, and weary wing,
    Our precious birdling lay.

And now, a fresh, green baby-grave,
    Out in the still, cold air,
Holds his pale dust—the faded robe
    His freed soul used to wear.

A little life—a slender span,
    Made up of Summer hours,
Was all of him—he ope'd his eyes,
    And closed them with the flowers.

.

THE NOSE OUT OF JOINT.

INSCRIBED TO "EMILY."

I WAS a spoiled and petted thing,
　And "Baby" was the name.
By which my mother called to me,
　Till little brother came.

I used to have a cradle-bed
　Just made to suit my form,
Where sweet I slept "all by myself,"
　So nice, and snug, and warm.

And gentle nurse would walk with me
　In summer-time, where flowers
Of red, and white, and purple hue,
　Bloomed in their fragrant bowers.

When neighbors called and asked to see
  "The Darling," I was brought;
And many a nut and sugar-plum
  My eager fingers caught.

I had my little "party" scenes,
  And pleased I used to be,
For every toy my father brought
  Was always brought for me.

And yet I am not jealous now,
  Though times are not the same;
I had no mate to play with me,
  Till little brother came.

Although he has the cradle-bed
  That used to be my own,
Yet when I wake at morning now,
  I do not feel alone.

For well I know one little heart
  My childhood's joy partakes—

One little mouth will share my meal
Of slighted "thimble cakes."

He knows the language of my lips,
When fain I would command
Some pleasure which our good mamma
Nor nurse can understand.

And many a time his finger points,
In our sweet walks together,
To some bright flower I had not seen
Or bird of shining feather.

I would not be without him now,
Though times are not the same ;
I had no brother dear to love
Till little " Edwin" came.

A REMEMBERED SERMON.* •

It fell upon the ear like the rapt tones
Of Heavenly music, and the air around
Caught the sweet echo of the Pastor's words
All eloquent of love—the Saviour's love.
I cannot soon forget that face serene,
As, in the meekness of an humble trust,
It rose before us; there was such zeal
And earnest pleading in each look and tone.
No clamor of complaint for misdeeds done,
No fearful curse for duties unperformed,
No cry of threatening wrath,—but a sweet call
Of "mercy" to the wandering. "Brethren"—
He spoke, and every listening ear was bent
To catch each accent of his rich, clear voice,

* By Bishop Johns, of the Virginia Diocese.

10

As, from the open pages of The Book,
He read the simple language of his text,—
" The Master is come and calleth for thee."
They were such words as e'en a little child
Might have expressed as plainly, yet they fell
From those inspired lips-like melody;
And by each tone that followed, hearts were moved.
At length, the speaker's accents fervent grew,
As if the spirit of St. Paul was there
And spake again, through those meek, parted lips.
" Brethren," he said once more, " the Master's
        come."
Faith lifted up her bright, exulting eyes.
" Hail, Heavenly Visitor, at whose coming step
All gloomy shadows fade ; in the blest light
Of whose joy-giving smile, darkness and clouds
Must vanish.

          " Jesus, Redeemer, God,—Thou
At whose name the Cherubim bow down
And Angels veil their faces. Thou, whom the
        Heaven
Of Heavens cannot contain,—whose presence fills

Immensity,—dost Thou yet deign to choose
For thine abode, these earth-stained hearts of ours?
Oh, make them then by thine own cleansing grace,
Fit dwellings for so great and pure a Guest.
Banish from thence, dear Lord, all dross of sin,
And bless them with the light of holiness;
That when in judgment thy sure step draws near,
And Death proclaims in our dull, closing ear,
'The Master's come,' our yearning souls may cry,
In eager, glad response, 'Even so, come Thou,
Lord Jesus, come quickly.'"

\   *   *   *   *   *   *   *

I have heard eloquence in Senate halls,
Have seen men stirred to wrath, and moved to tears,
As mighty tongues chained listening multitudes,
By the grand utterance of noble thoughts.
I have bowed down to Genius as displayed
On glowing pages of immortal verse,
But never yet did my ear catch such tones
Of thrilling pathos as, that morning, fell
In burning words, from the inspired lips
Of that meek man of God.

"IN MEMORIAM."

(W. C. M—M.)

I HAD no thought when thou were with us here,
That I should write thy "In memoriam;"
That e'er this hand should, o'er a name so dear,
Trace that sad word, "departed."

      Where are words
To speak thy praise, oh, friend of noble soul?
What language shall my pen employ to tell
The thousand virtues that adorned thy life?
That life, whose brightening sun ne'er reached its
  noon.
The soldier falls upon the battle-field,
And muffled drum and martial music, slow,
Chime forth his requiem. The statesman dies,
And drooping banners wave above his bier,

While nations loud proclaim a nation's loss.
But ere the sculptured pile is reared, that marks
His grave, another takes his place, and fills
The vacant rank as well.

                         Not so with thee;
For in the hearts thou leav'st behind, there lives
The fadeless record of a good man's name.
And Memory calls, at mention of it,
Deeds, words, and smiles of kindness lost with thee.
Aye, Friendship loves to dwell on all thou wert—
Alas ! how few resemble thee, while none
Excel. So pure in heart, meek, gentle, mild,
Withal, of lofty aims, so emulous.
Thy manly heart throbbed but in unison
With truth and virtue ; noble thoughts there found
A fitting home, and love a sanctuary.
But Death disowns all greatness; and when Earth
Seemed fairest to thine eye, when Fortune smiled
And life's sky gleamed with rainbows—aye, when
      Love
Circled thy heart with its pure sympathies,
And thy proud cheek had but just lately felt

The thrilling sweetness of thy first-born's breath,
His icy dart was near thee. Slowly fell
The shaft that laid thee low; the fading cheek,
The brightening eye, the weary, laggard step,
All told that the Destroyer e'en would lay
A gentle hand on thee. The balmy airs
Of Southern climes were sought, alas! in vain.
Thou didst return with the Spring violets,
And, as they breathed sweet incense round thy bed,
God's Angel hushed thy breath, and laughing May
Awoke the flowers, to lift their heads, and smile
Above thy grave.

    Oh! it is well with thee,—
Well, for a soul like thine, thus to lay down
Earth's needful cross, and, early thus, put on
Heaven's waiting crown. To us, the way is dark,
Of thy dear presence and thy smile bereft;
Yet well we know that in life's conflict here,
Thine was, the while, a hero's noble part,
Thine now, a Conqueror's grave.

A MOTHER'S PRAYER.

GOD of Mercy! Father, Friend,
At thy feet we humbly bend;
Comfort, in our sorrow, send—
      Bless our little Willie.

Low he lies—his baby cheek
Fever-flushed, his eyelids meek
Closed in languor; Jesus, speak,
      Raise our little Willie!

Thou a parent's care hath known,
Thou a mother's love didst own.
Let our hearts to Thee make moan—
      Heal our little Willie.

Once to Thy kind bosom pressed,

Little ones were fondly blest ;
Soothe a troubled soul's unrest,
         Save our little Willie.

All day long his head hath lain
Restless from disease and pain—
Saviour, give him health again !
         Helpless little Willie.

Much of our life's dearest joy
Centres in him—angel boy ;
Do not our fond bliss destroy,
         Do not take our Willie.

But in mercy, God of power,
Spare, oh! spare this cherished flower,
Drooping in our home's sweet bower.
         Spare our little Willie !

Send, from Heaven's glad realm of light,
Messengers of love to-night ;
Let thine angels, pure and bright,
         Watch our little Willie.

And when morning comes to cheer,
Gracious Saviour, be thou near ;
Brighten hope and banish fear,
　　　　Heal our little Willie.

Or if it should be Thy will,
We would Thy stern law fulfil ;
Only whisper, " Peace, be still,"
　　　　Take our little Willie.

And above yon starry dome,
Where disease no more may come,
Let our darling find a home,
　　　　Angel little Willie !

TO SLEEP.

(WRITTEN IN SICKNESS.)

Touch me with thy soft hand,
Oh, gentle Soother of the weary-hearted;
   And bear me to that land
Where dreams restore the joys fore'er departed.

   Take from my brow this pain,
And from my heart its dull, cold weight of sorrow;
   Let me feel once again
Health, buoyant health, returning with the morrow.

   The daylight hath gone by,
Soft Night appears, her mystic shadows bringing;
   Seal with thy kiss mine eye,
And quench the tears from a full heart upspringing.

For though thy silent mien
Dost wear of Death perchance too close a seeming,
　　Yet in thy smile serene
I trace of quiet joy a welcomed gleaming.

　　Fold me to thy kind breast—
Already do I feel thy presence stealing
　　Near with its balm of rest—
Oh, lull to Lethean calm each rebel feeling.

　　And I will bless our God,
E'en while upon this couch of pain I languish,
　　That, fainting 'neath His rod,
Thy touch hath kindly soothed this fevered anguish.

　　Oh, once again draw nigh,
Bless the long, weary hours I still must number,
　　Seal with thy kiss mine eye—
Fold me to thy soft bosom, peaceful Slumber.

　　And when these aching eyes
Upon life's transient scenes are darkly closing,
　　May the freed spirit rise
To *endless rest* mid Heaven's own bliss reposing.

GONE HENCE.

(ON THE DEATH OF AN INFANT NEPHEW, WILLIE E. MEEM.)

Thou hast gone hence, my angel boy,
 Gone is thine eye's soft light;
The little form so fondly loved
 Hath vanished from our sight.

I see no more the smile that played
 Upon thy baby face;
No more, thy tiny arms reach out
 To meet my fond embrace.

Thy dimpled cheeks no more may press
 Thy mother's loving breast;
No more her voice in "lullaby"
 Hush thee to rosy rest.

The grave now hides, my precious boy,
 Thy fair, though faded mould,—

Thy little heart is pulseless now,
   Thy forehead, pale and cold.

And yet around us everywhere
   Are little things, that tell
Of all the joys we've lost in thee,—
   Joys loved, perhaps, too well.

Thy vacant cradle, carriage, chair,
   Thy mantle, toys, and ring,—
All, all are here to mock the tears
   Which tender memories bring.

But where thy infant step hath been,
   All now is grief and gloom;
And we, who watched thy baby glee,
   Are wailing round thy tomb.

Be still, my heart, why darkly mourn
   The beautiful and free;
Thou'lt not come back to us, my boy,
   Yet we may go to thee.

THE BRIDE OF DEATH.

(SUGGESTED BY THE DEATH OF A LADY SOON TO HAVE BECOME A
BRIDE.)

BRING flowers, bring snowy lilies fair,
    To twine around her brow,
For lo ! the young, the pure, the bright,
    In death is slumb'ring now.

Tread softly,—angels hover near,
    Their viewless wings outspread—
Bright visitants returned to Earth
    To watch around the dead.

How changed the home where *she* hath moved,
    The blessing and the pride
Of loving hearts, that struggle now
    Their helpless grief to hide.

But yesterday, all bright with hope,
    Her voice in music burst;—
Alas! that in Death's phantom throng,
    Our fairest should be first.

Ah, broken is the golden chain
    Of hopes and memories dear,
That hung around the cherished form
    Now slumb'ring on this bier.

And parted is the household band;
    All desolate and lone
They weep: from out the parent nest
    The sweetest bird hath flown.

Afar is heard the tearful wail
    Of love by hope denied;
He mourns for her, the doubly lost,
    Who would have been his bride.

The Orange blossoms faded lie,
    Culled for the bridal wreath;
Lay them aside,—with lily-bells
    Crown ye the Bride of Death.

TO A DEAR UNCLE.

(ON HIS DEPARTURE FOR CALIFORNIA.)

HEAVEN's blessing rest on thee, beloved,
    As to a distant land
Thou wand'rest far, while we remain,
    A broken household band.

The Summer birds will come and go—
    The flowers will bloom and fade;
The autumn winds sigh mournfully
    Amid the forest's shade.

And loving lips will call thy name
    In whispered accents low,
And yearning hearts will sigh for thee
    Wherever thou mayst go.

And yet thou'lt not return to us
   For many a weary day:
Spring's verdure, Summer's bloom will find
   The wand'rer still away.

And prayers will oft ascend for thee,
   At morn and eventide;
When gathered round the social hearth
   We miss thee from our side.

Ah, then in Memory's trace will come
   Thy well-remembered tone;
The look of kindness and the smile
   That's lost when thou art gone.

And at the board, the cheerful board,
   Which thou wert wont to share,
Hushed now will be the merry jest,
   Where sits thy vacant chair.

At evening too, when music rings
   Loud through the parlor hall,

When heard the song by thee loved best,
Tears will unbidden fall.

In Summer's glory, Winter's gloom,
　By hearth, and on the stair,
All day, at morning, noon, and night,
　We'll miss thee everywhere.

Nor will the gladness to our home
　Come back, our hearts to cheer,
Or mirth and glee return again,
　Beloved, till thou art here.

Then linger not too long away,
　Far in a distant land;
Remember that thou leav'st behind
　A lonely household band.

A FATHER'S LAMENT.

I CANNOT make thee dead, my child,
 I cannot make thee dead,
Although thy form lies cold and still
 Within its cradle-bed.

And on thy breast I see the flowers
 Of Summer, fragrant lie,
Like thee to breathe out their sweet life,
 And then, like thee, to die.

Meet emblems they, of thy brief span,
 So joyous, calm, and free,—
No cloud to dim, no blight to stain
 Thy soul's sweet purity.

I gaze upon thy little form,
 So motionless and cold;

And almost doubt that what I see
  Is but a lifeless mould.

Thy gentle eyes seem closed in sleep,
  To ope again more bright,
I cannot feel, that quenched and gone
  Is their sweet spirit-light.

And in fond memory too, I see
  A sweet, bright, baby face,
Following me with its earnest gaze,
  And modest, winning grace.

How meekly o'er those little orbs
  The close-sealed eyelids lie,—
But when I speak, no soft tone comes
  Like music, in reply.

And when I press the tiny hand
  Near to my beating heart,
Its icy coldness makes the pulse
  Of warm affection start.

My child, how can we give thee up,
  Our Mary, sinless one!
Where will the gladness of our home
  Be now, thy smile is gone?

But yesterday, thy baby arms
  Reached out to welcome me;
And now, a soulless shrine of dust
  Is all I clasp of thee.

Oh God! who know'st a parent's love,
  Forgive, if, at Thy will,
Our hearts are crushed,—Thy mercy yet
  May whisper, " Peace—be still."

No longer may I pause to hear,
  In prattling accents sweet,
The voice whose baby tones were first
  My coming step to greet.

Yet well I know that in that clime
  Where all is light and love,

Close in the Saviour's tender breast
  Nestles our timid Dove.

And though thou never more mayst come
  To us, yet we may go
To thee, sweet baby, when the cares
  And griefs of life are o'er.

Now fare thee well, my angel child,
  Henceforth there'll surely be
Between our hearts and Heaven, a chain
  Linking us still with thee.

One kiss upon the marble cheek,
  Then to the arms of God
We yield thee, while, with chastened hearts,
  We bow beneath His rod.

No more with gladness thy dear smile
  Our home and hearts may fill,
Yet in the mansions of the blest
  Thou art "*our* Mary" still.

And 'mid Heaven's radiant Cherub-hosts
  Thy little face, so fair,
Will be, when we are called above,
  The first to meet us there.

Oh, from that land of fadeless bloom,
  Where thou art wandering now,
With no disease to mar the light
  That shines upon thy brow,

Look on us, baby, still, and be
  The guardian Angel given,
To guide our faltering, wayward steps
  From this dull Earth to Heaven.

NIGHT-WATCH WITH A DEAD INFANT.

(INSCRIBED TO MR. AND MRS. DEXTER OTEY, OF LYNCHBURG.)

TREAD softly here!—Upon this little couch
An angel sleeps. Closed are its eyes, and cold
Its forehead fair, yet on the lip Heaven's seal
Of holiest love is placed,—a Cherub smile.
Upon the breast, so still and quiet now,
The little hands are folded peacefully;
And the young heart will throb again no more
In restless agony.

           This was a flower
Of rare and winning loveliness; 'twas reared
And watched and tended with devoted care;
But when it learned to know the voice of love,
And to give back affection's fragrance—lo!

The Spoiler came, and with his canker-touch
Blighted the tender blossom, till it fell
Withered and crushed from off the parent stem.
Angel hands caught up the faded floweret,
And afar to Heaven's immortal bowers
Bore it with gentle care, to live and bloom
Mid the soft genial airs of Paradise.
There, falls no blighting breath upon the flowers,
And there, no shadowy veil shuts from our gaze
The forms we love. In that bright radiant realm
Of endless joy and sunshine, wanders now
The little sinless soul, o'er whose pale shrine
We keep this midnight vigil. Angel child!
Methinks I see thee in that Eden clime
Of glowing light and beauty. On thy brow,
So cold and pallid here, no trace is there
Of suffering or disease,—no quick-drawn sigh,
No labored, panting breath, tells me of pain
That mocks all human skill, and makes the prayer
Wrung from parental lips wild in its tone
Of fervor and of anguish. Cherub hands
Crown thee with garlands now, and round thee bloom

12

Fadeless exotics, o'er whose shining leaves
Comes no decay.   Never, ah, nevermore
Shall thy bright eyes close in dull languor, or
Thy baby cheek flush with disease.   O'er fields
And pastures green, thy tiny feet are led
Near the still waters of the Better Land,
And the Good Shepherd takes thee in His arms
And folds thee to His bosom tenderly.
All night long I've watched beside thee, Mary,
And the hours have brought me holy musings
Of that bliss the freed soul must enjoy, when
Like a bird held captive from its own green
Forest bowers, it bursts, at length, the bars
'Gainst which its weary wing has fluttered long
And helplessly, and soaring high above
All storm, pours forth its warbling hymn of praise,
And love, and joyous thankfulness to Him
Who gave it liberty.   'Tis thus with thee.
And now as morning breaks o'er earth, and through
The window-casement daylight peers again,
I'll kiss once more thy dust and say to thee,
"Farewell, sweet babe, farewell!"   Thy home is now

Where only the " pure in heart" may hope to dwell;
I thank my God that He has called thee hence,
And I would fain follow, in humble trust,
The path of Truth, which leads to Heaven and thee.

THE SOLDIER'S DREAM.

FROM A PICTURE.

WHILE o'er the bloody field night's shadows crept,
A weary soldier on the green turf slept;
One arm his gun still clasping in his rest,
The other thrown across his brave, young breast,
With limbs worn down by all the toils of war,
His spirit in his slumber wandered far.

He had a dream,—'twas of his far-off home,
To which all crowned with honors he had come:
He felt his wife's embrace, his infant's kiss,
And his soul revelled in the envied bliss,—
For which he had so toiled and fought, and borne
All the privations which his frame had worn.

IIis favorite spaniel came his step to greet,
And played and gambolled round his dust-worn feet;
Each kind domestic smiled his voice to hear,
And poured their gladdening welcomes in his car.
Shrub, tree, and flower, as they met his sight,
Made him forget awhile his Country's fight.

Sleep on, brave soldier! morn will come again,
And bring to thy glad heart, distress and pain;
Thou'lt know that joys which now so real seem,
Are but the sweet delusions of a dream.
And 'mid the angry Cannons' deepening roar,
Those voices of thy home thou'lt hear no more.

CHILDREN.

Happy children! Heaven bless them;
  Every day I chance to meet
Pleasant, cheerful, smiling faces,
  Passing by me in the street.

Everywhere I meet glad children,
  Hurrying on with busy feet;
Little thinking, little caring,
  How I love their steps to greet.

Noble lads and "bonnie lassies,"
  School-room truants, loitering, slow,
Conning, absently, the lessons
  Which they "fear" they will not know.

Smiling girls,—confiding creatures,
  Telling "cronies," soft and low,

How their morning tasks were hindered
　By a favorite " College Beau."

And (how strange), no sooner mentioned,
　Than the Beau himself, is seen
Very gallantly proposing
　To escort,—the Books, I mean.

But I turn from lads and lassies,
　With their school-day hopes and fears,
With a prayer that life may spare them
　Sorrow's cup in later years.

Here are little ones, God bless them !
　Gaily tripping to and fro;
How like cherubs seem they,—only
　Wanting wings to make them so.

Laughing babies from the cradle,
　Closely hugged to nurses' arms ;
Little prattlers, tottling slowly,
　With their dainty " two year" charms.

Lisping accents! ah, how dearly
Do I love such tones to greet,
As I daily hear, in passing
Little children on the street.

Heaven must bless them, they are Heaven's:
Angels make them all their care;
And, as we are near to children,
Just so near to Heaven we are.

Who that sees their smiling faces,
Innocent, and pure, and mild,
Would not say, "My God, I thank thee,
I was once a little child."

STANZAS.

At early morn, from fragrant bowers,
With careless hand I gathered flowers;
Fresh with the zephyr's breath they grew,
A starry cluster bathed in dew,
Until from off their native stems
In eager haste I plucked the gems,—
Toyed with their perfumed leaves awhile,
An idle moment to beguile—
When in my path, lo! at midday,
A group of withered flow'rets lay:
Unlike the buds I plucked at morn,
Their dewy freshness faded, gone.
'Tis thus, thought I, in Youth's glad hours
We gather Time's joy-laden flowers,

And toying idly with his glass
We let the golden moments pass,
Till in Life's noonday path we tread,
On Hope's bright morning-glories dead;
Their freshness gone, we only see
The faded flowers of Memory.

LITTLE HELEN.

THEY tell me thou art dead, fair child,
　That on thy sweet, young brow,
The gloom and coldness of the grave
　Is resting darkly now.

That in this world where thou didst move
　As with an Angel's grace,
We never more may hope to meet
　Thy soul-lit, beaming face.

That hushed is now the voice, whose tone
　Brought gladness to the ear
Of fond Affection, while with us
　Its music lingered near.

And that the love which softly shone,
　So earnestly and bright,

From out the tender, spirit-depths
Of thine eyes' gentle light,

No more will bless us with its glance
Of sympathy so dear,
Which came, e'en like an Angel's smile,
Our yearning hearts to cheer.

Alas! alas! we dreamed not, on
That sad remembered day,
When in her snowy, flower-strewn shroud
Thy Baby-Sister lay,

That thou, of that bereavèd band
Whose tears fell fast and long
Upon her breast, would be the next
To join the Angel throng.

That thou, though fairest, would be first
To greet her in that clime,
Where moments are not measured
By the falling sands of Time.

Nor did we dream when in the grave
  We laid her form so low,
The dust upon her marble cheek,
  Death's seal upon her brow,

That ere one month should fill its course,
  Thou too wouldst sink to rest,
Where Summer birds would sing all day,
  Above thy silent breast.

Ah, vain is human love, and vain
  The dearest joys of Earth,
Since hopes that seem to us most fair,
  Thus perish in their birth.

Thy life, sweet child, was like the blush
  That lingers on the flower,
And only yields its perfumed tint
  At morning's dewy hour.

Thy soul, thy stainless, cherub soul,
  Could rest no longer here ;

It pined in Earth's dull, cheerless soil,
   For Heaven's more genial sphere.

And there I know that thou art blest
   Far more than thou couldst be
With us, e'en with the deep, wild love
   That blindly mourns for thee.

Where thou art, Helen, all is bliss;
   No clouds in darkness rise
To mar the light that shines around
   Thy pathway in the skies.

Oh, from that radiant spirit-clime,
   Look still in pitying love
On those thy parting hath bereft,
   Dear, cherished, household Dove.

And when God's messenger shall come
   Their spirits to release,
Be thine the angel hand to close
   Their weary eyes in peace.

THE CONFIRMATION.

THE night was calm and beautiful.   The Stars,
The quiet Stars, looked down with gentle eyes
On Nature's sleeping loveliness.   The flowers,
Those dewy gems that shine on Earth's fair breast,
Were nodding dreamily upon their stems ;
While the hushed zephyrs slumbered peacefully
Within their bosoms.   All around breathed tones
Of soft subduing melody, stilling
To quiet peace, the clamorous discord
Of man's jarring nature.

                              By the might
Of Sabbath influences, solemn, deep,
Our steps were guided willingly, to where
Both love and duty beckoned them,—the House
Of God.   A brooding stillness reigned within

His Temple. Hearts were raised to Heaven, lips
Hushed in prayerful silence, while around
The sacred Chancel knelt the little band
Of suppliants for grace. Manhood there bowed
His lofty head, and meekly asked of long-
Neglected Mercy, strength—to finish out
The remnant of his days, a soldier of
The Cross. Youth offered up the morning bloom
And freshness of its heart to Heaven, and prayed
For aid to conquer all temptation, and
To keep a strict, close walk with God. Childhood,
With Childhood's trust, begged wisdom of our
        Father,
And Orphanage bespoke protection of
His love.

Widowhood was there, with broken heart
And tearful eyes, pleading for meek submission
To His will. Sadness and joy commingled
Sympathy. Hope's glad, expectant bosom
Throbbed beside the pulse of Disappointment.
Happiness, that bright boon of young natures,

Touched the sombre garb of Sorrow. Innocence
Bowed down, with sage Experience.

One common goal
Had brought their several paths this night
Together, and in God's pure sight, their wants
And pious claims were equal. Oh 'twas sweet
To see the holy man approach them near,
And "laying hands" on each, ask listening Heaven
For blessings on them all.

Doubt, lingering by
With timid footstep, tearfully embraced
Faith's proffered blessing. Penitence bowed down
In meek humility, and from his heart
Arose sweet incense of devotion. To
The Sinner's ear, there came sad tones of low
And earnest pleading. Would he longer strive
Against God's waiting Spirit? Would he still
Delay, even while that voice yet lingered
In his ear, which oft before, as now, had
Whispered, "Son, give me thy heart?"

                      Ah, never,
Nevermore, perhaps, to him may come its
Sweet, remembered music,—nevermore the
Kind assurance heard, " Ask, and it shall be
Given,—seek, ye shall find,—knock, and it shall
Be opened unto thee."   *   *   *   *

*   *   *   *   *   Oh, may our souls
No solace find, in this dim, tearful vale,
Till, shaking off Transgression's fetter, we
May all approach our Father's Mercy-seat;
And listening Seraphs, waiting round, may catch
From our full hearts, and bear to Heaven's glad ear
The cry, " Oh Lord,—we come !"

TO A SLEEPING INFANT.

LITTLE one, with eyelids closing
　　Softly to their wonted rest,
In thy mother's arms reposing,
　　Folded gently to her breast—

Say, what visions, brightly glowing,
　　Float before thy slumbering eye,
On thy heart rich dreams bestowing
　　Of that world beyond the sky?

Dost thou view the crystal river,
　　Sparkling clear through meadows green;
Wanderest thou where dew-gems quiver
　　Mid the flowers of golden sheen?

Lo ! a smile—I know its meaning—
   Angel forms communion keep ;
Spirits from on high are gleaning
   Secrets from thee, in thy sleep.

They are asking, sinless darling,
   Of the path untried and new,—
Whether here so bright a starling
   May to Heaven's high cause be true.

List their message—o'er thee bending,
   Hear them in low whispers say :
" Lean on God, His truth attending,
   Nought shall harm thee on thy way.

" Life is but a wavelet, shaken
   By a storm from wintry skies ;
At its close thine eyes shall waken
   In their native Paradise."

ON THE DEATH OF MRS. FANNIE S. GIBBONS,

OF HARRISONBURG, VIRGINIA.

THE breath of Spring is nigh—it comes once more
  To glad the Earth where Winter's frown hath
    been,
And violets their fragrant incense pour
  On flowery paths, through dewy meadows green;
But all in vain they smile for us—we mourn
For *thee*, sweet Blossom, from our bosoms torn.

The birds, gay warblers, flit from tree to tree,
  Waking glad melody in forest bowers,
And laughing brooks flow on in sportive glee—
  While sunshine crowns the swiftly-passing hours;
Alas! *we* heed them not: Death's form hath passed
In at our threshold, since we saw them last.

And thou, with love's high hopes fresh in thy heart,
   Joy's smile, like sunlight, on thy fair, young
      brow,
Thou wert the prize won by his cruel dart;
   Thine the dear form his ruthless hand laid low—
Oh, ne'er before hath his cold fingers pressed
Their frozen clasp around a purer breast.

Thine was a spirit pure as Summer rose,
   When morning wakes its fresh, young leaves to
      light,
And in thy heart Affection found repose,
   While holy thoughts there nestled, warm and
      bright,
But, like the lily, which rude storms have tried,
Thou bow'dst thy lovely head and meekly died.

Yes, *thou art dead!* Deep, deep the sod, beneath
   Whence Summer violets spring, thou'rt sleeping
     low.
Say, wilt thou not return when May's soft breath
   O'er timid buds and meek-eyed flow'rets blow?

Ah, vain these bitter tears, and vain the prayer
Affection murmurs in its wild despair.

Thou'lt not come back to us, though early flowers
    Still pour their fragrance on the balmy air ;
Though warbling birds make glad Earth's lonely
        bowers,
    We'll miss *thy* voice, dear lost one, everywhere ;
Yet Faith will whisper, in low accents sweet,
" There is a clime above, where we may meet."

Oh, from that land of never-fading bloom,
    Still bend on us, dear one, thy pitying gaze,
While from the darkness of thy early tomb
    We humbly strive our yearning thoughts to raise ;
Hover around us, Angel-guide, till we
Shall quit this world to live again with thee.

ASPIRATIONS.

Rouse thee, my soul, wake all thy slumbering
    powers,
Nor longer trail thy pinions in the dust,—
Bright aims, high purposes, demand thy zeal;
Upward and soar ! thou who canst dare to claim
That richest heritage, a spirit-birth.
What are the sordid gains for which they toil,
Whose highest guerdon is the world's poor praise?
What is ambition, wealth, or even fame,
But empty bubbles broken by a breath?
These do but mock thy cravings; put thee on
Faith's burnished helmet, Truth's unfailing shield,
And gird thee with new hope and trusting love,
And patient, firm endurance; look aloft,
And not to self alone devote thy powers;
Live not for self alone.

Let others seek
In hidden treasures of the Earth and Sea,
That paltry, perishable thing called gold.
Aye, let them toil, as many do full oft,
With aching heart and brow to win a name;
Or let them grasp at *power*, to learn that crowns
May *press* the brow which wears them.   Not for
    thee
These glittering baubles, not for thee, my soul.
Earth is thy battle-ground, Heaven thy fair home;
Strive to obtain a victor's welcome there.
Live for mankind, thy Country—more than all,
Live for thy God, my Soul.

L'ENVOI.

(FROM "IMOGEN," AN UNFINISHED POEM.)

I HAVE been out, dear Love, this radiant morning,
In the broad open field and wild wood near;
Amid whose vocal shades and sunlit meadows
We took our last sweet walk, when thou wert
here.
The Sun shone clear as then, the air was balmy,
The while a quiet breeze played o'er the hill;
And yet my heart was joyless, love, and lonely,
The music in my bosom hushed and still.
I could not heed the warbling matin-chorus,
Which, from a thousand throats, went up on
high;
Nor did I mark, as then, the low, sweet humming
Of each glad insect, as it murmured by.

Sad memories of sad things bowed down my spirit,
    And dimmed mine eyes to Nature's charms
        around,—
Cold, cruel tones, and colder words of parting,
    Blent in strange discord with each vocal sound.
Ah! Love and Change, ye have a mystic meaning,
    Which only they who know ye *both* can tell.
With me Love ne'er could know such cold estrange-
        ment,
    Or Friendship even breathe such cold farewell.
    *   *   *   *   *   *   *   *
Rememberest thou, that 'tis the mild September,
    That month to Memory and to Love so dear;
Why is it then, at this sweet, hallowed season,
    I vainly pause thy coming step to hear?
Thou shouldst be with me,—we should roam together
    The tangled pathways of the forest dim,
Together pause, as oft of yore, to listen,
    As Nature upward sends her choral hymn.
Yet if life offers thee more joy in absence,
    And thou more happy art, when far away,
I'll welcome loneliness always, and sorrow,
    To know that thou art always glad and gay.

THE WOODS IN SUMMER.

THE woods, the woods! ah, what delicious calm
Their freshness brings.   Once, with a fevered pulse
And weary heart, I sought these cooling shades,
And by this flowing rill, so clear and bright,
I sat me down in very weariness.
It was a day of loveliness, in June,
When Nature seemed dressed for a holiday,
And little children welcomed it with joy,—
Tossing with busy hands the new-mown hay,
Or wreathing garlands of the sweet, wild flowers,
While bird and bee chorused each merry peal
Of ringing laughter.   All the air around
Echoed the hum of voices—every breeze
Wafting a breath of incense, pure and sweet,
And blooming fields of yellow, waving grain,
Laughed in the golden sunlight.

To the woods

I wandered then, as now, with saddened heart,
And 'mid these rural shades found sweet repose.
Ah, it is well, sometimes, to turn aside
From all the foot-worn paths of busy life,
And seek a respite from its clamorous toil
Amid the hush of solitude like this;
To hear no sound save that of murmuring rill,
Or foaming cascade leaping to the light,
Or, now and then, the squirrel's lonely chirp
Blending in chorus with the wild bird's note;—
Anon the sigh of zephyrs, low and sweet,
As o'er us waves the leafy canopy,
Fraught with their perfumed breath. To watch the
        while,
Through trembling boughs, the calm, blue, smiling
        sky,
And think of those who early walked with us
Life's changeful paths beneath it; whose blest feet
Now press the "golden streets" beyond. How
        sweet,
Amid such scenes as this, to wander o'er

14*

Our childhood's faded track, and dream again
Of pleasant rambles through the forests wild,
With playmates, young and fair—in every tone
To catch an echo dim of "Auld Lang Syne;"
To trace in every leaf and flower His smile,
Whose hand divine hath made them—aye, to hear
In running brook and foaming torrent wild,
The great voice of our Father.

                    It is thus
The woods, the sweet, calm summer woods, become
The trysting place for Memory and Hope ;
While Faith, the meek-eyed angel, waiting near,
Unfolds to each the antitype of God.

TO MY HARP.

CHERISHED harp, my soul is saddened,
  Nought can soothe like thy sweet strains ;
Though so long thy chords have slumbered,
  I'll awake their tones again.

Tears I've shed since last we parted,
  Burning tears of grief and pain,—
Hopes I fondly nursed have perished,
  Nevermore to bloom again.

Once, thy notes of rapture thrilled me,
  Now there's wailing in thy tone ;
And thy trembling strings, forsaken,
  Answer to the wind's low moan.

Gentle harp, I know thy meaning,
  For my soul hath felt the spell

Left of loneliness and sorrow
　　By that parting word, " farewell.'

Once a form of matchless beauty,
　　O'er thee swept a skilful hand,
And a voice of thrilling sweetness
　　Did thy gentle tones command.

But that form, so fondly cherished,
　　Ne'er shall know thee as of yore ;
And that voice, so sweet, shall waken
　　To thy gladdening strains no more.

Heavenly spirit ! stoop and hover
　　Near me, as I touch these strings,—
Catch the prayer my lips shall murmur,
　　Waft it on thy angel wings.

When my soul, no longer fettered,
　　Is from Earth's dull bondage free,
May we strike our harps together
　　In a bright Eternity.

THE CHRISTENING.

A LITTLE cherub-band, in snow-white robes,
Were offered at the chancel.   Loving eyes
Watched tenderly each smiling face, and arms
Of fond affection circled them.   They gazed
In wonder now, first on the Pastor's face,
And then upon the Font inquiringly,
As though they fain would ask what mystic grace
Lay hidden in those glistening drops for them.
Lo! as the Man of God lifts up his voice
To ask of Heaven its blessing, close they cling
In helpless weakness to the yearning breasts
That throb for them with parent sympathy.
And as he takes each, in his pastoral arms,
They timidly shrink back as half afraid,
Then to his kindly bosom nestle close.
Now as he lays his hand upon their brows,

And with a solemn mien closes the rite
Which pledges them to Heaven, Angels pause
To hear the vow of consecration—bend
To seal it with a kiss, and lo! a smile
Stamps the impression on each beaming face.
Ye sinless little ones, in after years,
When worldly snares are set for your weak steps,
And Pleasure's siren tones call to allure
Your hearts from virtue, when perchance the arms
Which clasp you now, are folded stiff in Death—
Hark then! "a still small voice" will softly breathe
Into your ear this truth : that while the dew
Of childhood innocence lay fresh upon
Your hearts, *Love* brought you here and offered you
To Jesus. Let that memory suffice
To keep you ever in the path of Truth;
And when at last ye shall lie down to rest
Within your narrow beds, may dewy flowers
Spring over breasts *which never lost in life*
The pearl of their baptismal purity.

GIVE ME THY BLESSING, FATHER DEAR.

Give me thy blessing, father dear!
  On this, my bridal eve;
Oh, let me from thy tender lips
  Some whispered word receive.
Some accent spoken soft and low,
  In earnestness and love,
That e'er will linger in my heart,
  Its talisman to prove.
That heart is very sad to-day,
  Though bright the future seems,—
Our parting hour approaching,
  Throws a shadow o'er my dreams.
I think of all *thou'st been* to me,
  And fear lest, when I roam,

I may not find such changeless love
  As I have found at home.
Give me thy blessing, father dear!
  'Twill calm my troubled heart;
One only balm may soothe me now,—
  Thy blessing ere we part.

GUARDIAN SPIRITS.

[A beautiful feature in the Roman Catholic Faith, teaches that each one of us, while on earth, is watched over continually by a Guardian Spirit, whom Heaven appoints to direct and shield us; and that this viewless counsellor may, perchance, wear the form of some loved one who has "gone before" us to the Better Land.]

IT is a holy thought, that while we dwell,
O'ershadowed by the gathering clouds of Earth,
Each has an Angel friend, who follows near
On viewless wing, beside us, taking note
"Of thorns and briery places," "lest we dash
Our foot against a stone," or darkly grope
On Error's brink,—that Spirits, pure and bright,
Are ever speaking to us, though the tones
Of their mysterious voices are not heard.
They prompt to deeds of kindness, love, and truth,—
Alas, that we, so often fail to heed
Their silent whisperings.   They float around

15

On pinions light as air,—we ne'er may mark
The flutter of their wings, although, perchance,
They oft may wear the features we have loved.
A mother's eye, closed long ago, may beam
In their soft gaze; a father's arm may clasp
In their embrace; a sister's angel smile
Blend in their look of love; a brother's form,
Hid from us by the grave, may wander still
Beside us, as in other years, when life and hope
Were new.   Aye, it may be, that dimpled hands,
Which we saw folded in the clasp of Death,
Are beckoning to us now from that bright sphere
Where ne'er is seen a vacant cradle, where
The little suffering form o'er which we bowed
For days in agony, hath put aside
Its clay, and weareth now a Cherub's wings.
Babe, Sister, Mother, though I may not know
Who, of Love's buried trio, Heaven appoints
To guide my footsteps here, yet I have felt
New influences round life's pathway thrown
Since ye have entered the eternal gates.
Joy springs anew, as Faith breathes, low and sweet,
" Reunion there forever."

SUMMER'S GONE.

Ah! Summer's gone! The Autumn breezes sighing,
   Murmur its requiem, while a dirge-like moan
Comes from the heart, an echo dim, replying—
                " Summer's gone!"

Lo! in the forests faded leaves lie scattered,
   And sweet young blossoms of their freshness
      shorn,
And clinging vines that ruthless storms have shat-
  tered.
                Summer's gone!

Pale roses, 'neath the breath of Autumn stooping,
   Will lift their heads no more to greet the morn;
And lilies too, on slender stems are drooping—
                Summer's gone!

The song of birds is hushed mid vernal bowers;
　　The sportive butterfly, of sunlight born,
No more is seen to woo the gentle flowers,—
　　　　　　　　Summer's gone!

The fragrant freshness of the bright June weather,
　　July's warm glory, August's mellow dawn,—
All, all have passed, bird, bee and flower together.
　　　　　　　　Summer's gone!

And with it, too, how many a hope hath perished,
　　Leaving the joyous bosom sad and lone,—
Oh! where are now the day-dreams they once
　　　cherished?
　　　　　　　　Summer's gone!

Aye, though its coming throw an emerald glory
　　O'er this glad world, yet hark!—a triumph tone
From *our doomed cities** shouts the welcome story,
　　　　　　　　"Summer's gone!"

　　　　* Norfolk and Portsmouth, in 1855.

Yes, from thy homes, Virginia, smiles have vanished
  That greeted merrily Spring's rosy dawn,
From stricken hearts, joy hath fore'er been ban-
  ished;
                Summer's gone!

Gone, gone,—the Autumn breeze proclaims it,
  sighing,
While to the ear, there comes an echoing moan
From Hope's pale embers on Love's hearthstone
  lying,
                "Summer's gone!"

TO HER WHO ASKED ME FOR "A POEM."

WOULDST have a poem; dear one? ah! then look
Abroad this sunny morn on Nature's face,—
There, is true poetry in unmeasured lines,—
There God himself hath brightly pictured forth
His Glory and his Power. The mountains old,
In lofty grandeur rear their hoary crests
To meet the clouds. And yonder sky, so soft,
So calm, so clear, so beautiful, seems made
For eyes like yours to gaze on—eyes that see
No sombre hues in aught—to which indeed
Life's darker scenes are veiled—which only view
Through Hope's gay prism-glass those rainbow
        tints
That bless the gaze of Innocence. Behold!—
The world is full of poetry,—its herd
Of breathing forms, its busy insect life,

Its clouds, its storms, its sunshine, Day and
    Night,—
Its changing seasons all,—the smiling Spring
In her rich garniture of buds and flowers,—
Glad Summer with her joyous harvest-time,
Sweet meek-eyed Autumn with her plenteous stores
Of golden fruits—her mild October sun—
Her scarlet leaves and berries. Winter, too,
With his cold breath and glittering icicles—
His ermine robe of snow—his Christmas chimes,—
Each is within itself a poem true,
And God the glorious Author. Thine own heart,
My gentle friend, thy young, gay, careless heart,
Is but another poem, rich and rare,
In voiceless thought and tuneful numbers.
Ah! let its study be thy earliest care;
So "prune" its "rougher lines,"—so guard its
    truth,
That, when at last thy silent pulses tell
The volume closed, Truth, like a "critic" kind,
May, o'er thy Life's bright pages, justly write
That envied sentence,—"Beautiful!"

MY LITTLE FLOWER.

It was a rosebud, pure and sweet,
  That blossomed in the Spring;
And to my heart I fondly pressed
  The little winsome thing.

I loved it for its fragile form,
  And for a brow, so fair,—
It seemed a glistening pearl, half hid
  By waves of shining hair.

I loved it for an eye of blue,
  That on me softly shone;
But I have thought I loved it most
  Because—it was "my own."

So closely with my being, did
  This flower of beauty twine,

That soon my thankless mother-heart
Became an Idol-shrine.

And God, who lent the bud of love,
Called back to Heaven his own ;
Death kissed it sleeping, and no more
Its soft eyes on me shone.

Ah ! well do I remember now
The little winsome thing ;
It was a rosebud, pure and sweet,
That perished in the Spring.

TO THE WIND.

WHAT wouldst thou teach us by thy murmurs low,
Oh, melancholy Wind?—what message bear,
In the deep cadence of thy mournful voice,
From the Eternal sphere? We know thou hast
Some mission pure, for thou receivedst thy tones
From Him whose will the elements obey;
Thou speakst of Him in every murmuring sigh
That's wafted from thy breath, and oft I seem
To hear His voice in thine, mysterious Wind!
Surely a magic power is given to thee,
For thou dost sometimes wear the zephyr's form,
Bringing to flowers soft airs, from sunny climes;
Then, with one touch of thy strange, mighty wand,
The dew is scattered from the lily's cup,
And sunbeams take its place. Thou dalliest near
The violet's bed, and lo! it wakes to light—

Seeking some sheltered nook, or mossy dell,
Wherein to breathe its sweet young life away.
Capricious Wind!—by one rude kiss of thine,
I've seen the woodbine trailing in the dust,
And proud oaks bend, to own thy tyrant power;
Aye more, the very waves are made to roll
Obedient to thy sway. Afar from home
The mariner counts thee his foe or friend,
For, of his loss or gain, thou seem'st to be
Heaven's instrument.

What is thy form, and what
The mien thou wearest? Sometimes, in lonely hours,
I've fancied thee a spirit, and have held
Communion with thee oft; half hoping then
That thou wouldst yet disclose the features fair
Of some departed face. But this I know
Was love's vain fantasy. Thy form and place—
None know save our Father. He "tempers thee
To the shorn lamb;" and I will be content
To hear thy music tones, and humbly blend
My voice of grateful praise with thine, oh Wind!

A CHILD'S MORNING HYMN.

FATHER in Heaven! I rise once more
　With morning's cheerful light,
To thank Thee for Thy watchful care
　Throughout the long, long night.

Thy goodness kept me safe from harm
　While darkness round me lay,
And to Thy faithful service now
　I consecrate this day.

Let every thought my heart employs
　Be pleasing in Thy sight;
And may Thy gracious eye behold
　Each action with delight.

Preserve my lips from sinful speech,
　My heart from evil free;

Since all I think, or say, or do,
    Is known, my God, to Thee.

Bless with Thy love my parents dear,
    My sisters, brothers kind;
Let all who seek to know Thy truth
    That heavenly knowledge find.

Bless too, the poor, the rich, the great,
    The sick, the bond, the free;
And may the Heathen souls be taught
    To worship only Thee.

Throughout life's everchanging scenes
    Be Thou my constant friend;
From aught that could my soul deceive
    Preserve me to the end.

And when from Earth I pass away
    In Death's severe embrace,
Father! oh, may I then enjoy
    Thy presence "face to face."

16

THE BLIND GIRL WITH FLOWERS.

(FROM A PAINTING BY LEUTZE.)

Oh! I could sit for hours
And gaze upon the placid beauty of thy fair, young
  face,
Sweet child of Night. There is a spell of quiet
  holiness
Upon thy brow, as if thy God had placed a seal
  thereon,
Marking thee out as something that the obtrusive
  hand of harm
And guilt must touch not.
                                        Round
Thy close-sealed eye a shade of sadness lingers, yet
  there's nought
Of restless murmuring at thy darkened lot—no
  sombre trace

Of dull repining at the will of Heaven.   There is a
    calm
Of pious resignation sadly sweet, and throwing o'er
Thy veiled and sightless orbs, a halo pure and
    lovely
As thy dreams of Light.
What were thy thoughts, oh! gentle one, what were
    thy thoughts of all
The glorious things that gladden earth, the sunlight,
    stars, and flowers ?
What thy dreams of rainbow, cloud, and mountain ?
    Had the meadow's
Quiet stream no charm for thee, save the low mur-
    muring music
Of its flow? the garden gems no varied form or
    color ?
Ah, thou lov'dst the flowers, for thy rounded arm
    now clasps a vase
Of gorgeous buds and blossoms, and thy curtained
    eyes are bent
As wont to catch one faint gleam at their loveli-
    ness.   Alas !

A lonely lot was thine, yet well I know thy soul
    had sweet
Revealings of that radiant clime, where Heaven's
    own cloudless light
Would charm thy raptured vision, where thy lyre
    no more attuned
To sadness, would awake its tones of holy joy, that
    thus
The very earliest ray that ever blest thy being,
    shone
Direct from God.

"WE HAD BUT ONE."

We had but one—her little life
  Seemed made of golden hours,
And each a gladness yielded, like
  The fragrant breath of flowers.

We had but one—her glowing smile
  Of innocence and mirth,
Shone like a star in wintry skies,
  Around our lonely hearth.

We had but one—her angel voice
  In baby accents heard,
Still falls upon my listening ear
  Like sweetest song of bird.

We had but one—how sweet the task
    For Love's fulfilment given,—
Daily to watch the expanding flower,
    And keep it pure for Heaven.

How sweet, through coming years, to guide
    In Truth's unerring way,
Her gentle heart, that Sin tempt not
    Its timid thoughts to stray.

And when her woman's course was run,—
    Kissing the chastening rod,
How sweet to close her eyes in peace,
    And yield her back to God.

Not thus, oh Father, hath it seemed
    Good in thy sight to be;
Long length of years was not for her,
    Nor Woman's destiny.

But let us not arraign Thy love
    In this dark hour of need;

Enough, Great God, to know Thou wilt
 Not break the bruised reed.

Our child is dead,—a wintry grave
 Holds now her precious clay,—
"Thy will be done—'twas thine to give,
 And thine to take away."

MEMORY.

Au ! I love to remember the days that are gone,
And the pleasures that brightened my life's early
    morn ;
When the world, bathed in sunlight from Hope's
    radiant skies,
Seemed a glad, fairy land to my joy-beaming eyes.

Now, alas ! the bright prism I saw it through then,
Has o'erdarkened its colors, again and again ;
I still gaze, but the rainbow tints silently fade,
And in hiding the sunlight, leave only the shade.

Yet despite the world's clamor, its turmoil and strife,
Some bright flowers will spring in the pathway of
    life ;

And the fairest to me are those blossoms that gleam
All along the green banks of fond Memory's stream.

They shine 'mid the vapory mists that arise
Like those sunbeams that glisten through showery
skies ;
And, whatever the future may bring us at last,
We've the fragrance still left of these flowers of the
Past.

Ah ! let us, then, seize the glad moments which fly,
To gather Love's flowers in our pathway that lie,
Since when all that is present lies dead in the past,
'Tis the chaplet of Memory that crowns us at last.

TO BABY FRANK, SLEEPING.

SLEEP on, baby, take thy rest
Calmly on thy mother's breast,
Slumber seal thy gentle eye,
While she sings thy " lullaby."

Sorrow cannot harm thee now,
Care nor anguish shade thy brow;
For thy heart is pure and free,
And thy pulse beats healthfully.

O'er thee bends a watchful eye,
Angel forms are hovering nigh—
Baby, thou art truly blest,
Pillowed on thy mother's breast.

May the future bring no night
To thy soul's unclouded light;
Ne'er sin's bitter, rankling dart,
Throw one shadow on thy heart.

But be all life's dreams as bright
As thy childhood's sleep was light,
Baby, mayst thou never know
Aught of sorrow, sin, or woe.

SHALL I BE FORGOTTEN THUS?

ON PASSING A NEGLECTED GRAVE BY THE WAYSIDE.

INSCRIBED TO THE LOVED ONES AT HOME.

Ah, shall I be forgotten thus, when I am dead,
Will not e'en a soft Daisy bloom over my head,
When these eyes have long closed in their visionless
    sleep,
Will not Love o'er my grave still a kind vigil keep?

Aye, and when the glad Spring comes with verdure
    and bloom,
Will not loving hands, tenderly, plant round my
    tomb
Bright Roses and Woodbine, and meek Violets
    blue,
Ever loving them best, because I loved them too.

Say, will *you* not then come, at the soft twilight
    hour,
And wander awhile through the lonely Death-bower
Where sleeps my pale form, still and cold in its
    rest,
Low down 'mid the gloom of the grave's silent
    breast?

Ah, then, as with soft timid footsteps you tread
On the turf which so mournfully covers my head,
Forget all the faults which the vanished life knew,
And think only, the heart once beat warmly for you.

Though parted the link in your glad household
    chain,
Thus let Memory's clasp reunite us again,
And her soft, gentle whispers call up from the past
Those glad moments of joy which death could not
    o'ercast.

17

The bright days of our childhood, when, joyous and
    free,
We roamed through the wildwood, for blossom and
    bee,
Or, lingering, knelt by the brook's tiny wave,
In its silvery ripples our bosoms to lave.

And won't you recall, too, the raptures we knew
When the first violets lifted their heads to the dew,
And the glad birds came back from their green
    Southern bowers,
As the Spring waked to light the long-slumbering
    flowers?

Ah, then, do not forget me thus, loved ones and
    true,
When hath faded the sound of my dying adieu;
Aye, though parted the link in your glad household
    chain,
Still let Memory's clasp reunite us again.

WAKE UP, LITTLE DARLING.

(TO ONE WHO WILL UNDERSTAND IT.)

WAKE up, little darling, the Sun is awake,
   And has taken his place in the sky ;
Even now, the sweet flowers are opening their
     leaves
   To the light of his radiant eye.

Wake up—all the blossoms and buds are awake,
   And the meadow is covered with dew,
But the bees are not chasing the butterflies yet,
   They are waiting, I dare say, for you.

Wake up—the sweet birds are awake, for I hear
   From a thousand gay flutterers nigh,
Glad matins of praise, like a chorus of love,
   Floating up to the Ruler on high.

Wake up; you are losing the bloom on your cheek,
 And the bright morn is hastening away,
All other glad things are awake and astir,
 Ah! then, why will Mary delay?

Up, up to your books, while the birds are about,
 They are busy e'en now in the bowers,—
Learn a lesson of industry, darling, from them,
 And be gentle and pure like the flowers.

TO AN ANGEL-SPIRIT.*

I SADDEN at thy mem'ry, darling child,
As thoughts of thy dark fate, thy painful doom,
Come up before me now,—dread picturings
Of agony and death. Thy slumbers deep,
So sweet and tranquil, full of angel-dreams,
And then the fearful wakening!—senses lost
In wild bewildering terror, as the flames
Hissed around thy pillow angrily. Thy look
Of dread surprise to find thyself alone,
And then thy piteous cry for "*Help!*"

Ah, could
Thy mother's arm have clasped thee then, or had

* Mary, only daughter of Dr. Gilmer, of Lynchburg, Va.,—
the recollection of whose melancholy fate is still painfully fresh
in the minds of her many friends.

Her voice been near to whisper courage, thou
Mightst yet have dared the window's height, and
    leapt
To arms outstretched to save thee.   But the while
She kept a midnight watch in her lone home,
Over thy baby-brother, shedding tears,—
Such tears as only fall from loving eyes,—
And mingling them with prayer, that God would
    smile
Upon her cradled boy, and give him health,—
She little dreamed that thou, her bright-eyed child,
Her gentle daughter, at that very hour
Wrestled with Death by fire !

               Tell us, Angel-child,
What thoughts came to thee in that fearful hour,
Of home and friends, and "mother."   Did *her*
    name,
Coupled with that of God, go up to swell
Thy martyr-shrieks of agony?   Did scenes
Of bygone blessings thou shouldst know no more,—
Thy father's features and thy brother's smile,

Float in thy visions? or didst thou breathe again
The little prayer, learned at thy mother's knee,
Which lingered on thy lips as sleep that night
Stole gently o'er thine eyelids? Didst thou say
" Our Father?" wilder sobbing forth the words
"Thy will be done!" and as the approaching flames
Drew near and nearer, piercing the red night,
With a most piteous cry, " *Deliver me*
From evil?"

         Ah, we may not know how passed
Those awful moments with thee—but we know
That ere the stars had paled in the soft sky,
Or night withdrawn her mantle from the earth,
That prayer was answered. Daylight saw thy form
Consumed to ashes,—Death had done his work,
And thy pure soul had entered its new life ;
For Christ the Lord had taken it to dwell
Henceforth with Him.

         Oh, it was better thus
To enter Heaven through a gate of fire

With soul untainted, and with childhood's dew
Yet resting on the heart, than live to see
Thine innocence depart with length of years.
Belovèd child, thy fate to us seems dark,
And fond lips breathe thy name mid gushing tears;
Yet there will come a time (God's purposes
Revealed), when we will say of thee, "'*Tis well*,"—
And Angels shall respond, "YEA, IT IS WELL."

A WELCOME.

TO THE MT. AIRY HOUSEHOLD AND GUESTS, WHO VISITED CLIFF

COTTAGE IN THE SUMMER OF 1858.

HARK, 'tis heard in sunny glades
  Glowing with delight,—
Glad with merry song of birds,
  Musical and bright.

Welcome to our valley fair,
  And to our mountains old,
Where Nature's gentlest charms are blent
  With loftiest grandeur bold.

Welcome to our whispering woods,
  And to our fields so fair,
Where sweetest voices, chiming, fill
  The glowing summer air.

Welcome, list, the echo flies ;—
　　Each passing zephyr bends
To catch the sound, whose murmur breathes
　　A welcome to you, friends.

E'en timid flowers look meekly up,
　　As eager to prolong
The joyous tone, while bird and bee
　　All share our welcome song.

Each beaming face, with rapture filled,
　　A gladness new imparts ;
Aye, welcome to our home and hearth,
　　Thrice welcome to our hearts.

TO A YOUNG SPARROW.

COME, little timid nestling, fear
    No danger, pray, from me;
I would not harm one feather which
    Our God hath given to thee.

I would not give thy downy wing
    One single stroke of pain;
I'd only guide thy wandering flight
    Back to the nest again.

Hark! now thy mother calls for thee
    In mournful chirping tone,
She knows not where, in this dim wood,
    Her little one hath flown.

I'll place thee where her watching eye
    May see thee with delight;
For well I know her fears have marked
    The coming of the night.

She thinks with terror and alarm
    Of " Pussy" lurking nigh,
With ready paw to seize thee when
    No rescuing hand is by.

Ah, oft do little ones like thee
    Give pain to parents dear,
By wandering from the path of right,
    With danger threatening near.

And little recking of the hearts
    That sigh for them in vain,
They rove, till conscience, like a guide,
    Conducts them back again.

This lesson teach them, little bird,—
    That though thy steps may stray,

Thou hast not *reason*, as *they* have,
To show thee wisdom's way.

And tell them that the same great hand
Which made both them and you,
Hath marked for each some destiny,
Your life long to pursue.

Ye both are objects of his care,
The creatures of his will;
Good children then should always strive
His wishes to fulfil.

Thy little warbling throat was made
His lofty praise to sing,
And he designed thy form to float
Through air, on lightsome wing.

Go then, thou little trembler, go—
Heaven's azure dome is thine;
Thou hast life's freedom, I its cares—
Thy Maker though is mine.

Why He hath differed thus, our paths,
We, finite, may not tell;
But this, I know,—He cannot err,
Who " *doeth all things well.*"

A CHILD'S EVENING HYMN.

As Day's bright splendor fades from view,
  And Night's dark shades appear,
Father in Heaven! low at Thy feet
  I once again draw near.

For all the blessings Thou hast strewn
  Around my path to-day,
I thank Thee, though, I know the least
  My praise can ne'er repay.

If I have sinned in word or deed,
  Or thought an evil thing;
Forgive, and let me sleep beneath
  The shelter of Thy wing.

Bless all I love, and let Thy grace
  Extend the wide world o'er,
Till every tongue shall speak Thy praise,
  And Thy great Name adore.

And when mine eyes shall close, to sleep
  Through Death's long, fearful night,
Father, oh, may I wake to see
  Thy face, in realms of light!

MUSINGS IN A CHURCHYARD.

I TOO shall die—the day will come
    I know not when, or where;
When stranger eyes will mark my grave
    Out in the still, soft air.

Yes, busy hands will heap the earth
    Above my silent breast,
Then careless turn to other tasks,
    And leave me to my rest.

I know not if the opening flowers
    Of Spring shall o'er me wave,
Or, if the Summer's fervid sun,
    Shall light my new-made grave.

18*

I know not if the Autumn winds,
   Their requiem tones shall sigh,
Or, if the Winter snows shall shroud
   The lone spot where I lie.

It may be at the morning hour,
   When Nature fairest seems,
And young hearts, gay with life and hope,
   Wake from their rosy dreams;

It may be when the setting Sun
   Lights up the parting day,
And little children homeward haste,
   From coming shadows gray,

That friendly hands will bear me out,
   And lay me calmly down,
To sleep my last, long, dreamless sleep,
   Low in the quiet ground.

It matters not—I shall not heed
   The scenes above my head,

Or know, when friendly footsteps pause
 Around my narrow bed.

I shall not heed the falling clods,
 That hide my slumbering clay,
Or mark when sad or careless eyes
 Turn from that mound away.

One wish I have,—that when I die,
 All earthly cares removed,
My sleep may be that blessèd sleep
 God giveth His beloved.

TO A REMEMBERED DREAM.

Come back, sweet dream, come back, and fill my
    spirit
With those bright, golden visions, flown too fast;
Not once, but oft come back, and float around me,
    Thou viewless guardian of the banished past.

Fond dream, beguiling to new life and gladness
    The buried memories of other years,
And thrilling with new joy my inmost being,
    Till slumber breaketh, and I wake—to tears.

When on life's sky I see no bow of promise,
    No golden sunlight gleaming o'er my way,
When all is gloom around, within, about me,
    And cold, and dark, and dreary, is my day:

Come then, bright dream, as darkness gathers
    round me,
And slumber soothes the sorrow-laden brow,
Unfold once more those visions of past hours,
    Glad moments, which I ne'er again may know.

Dear dream, come back, and cheer my weary spirit
    With Hope's bright golden visions, flown too fast;
Sleeping or waking, do thou float around me,
    Oh, guardian angel of the banished past.

THE STRICKEN HEART'S LAMENT.

[Written at the request of bereaved parents, to commemorate the mournful fate of a beloved child,—JAMES WARD (eldest son of James B. Ward, Esq., of Campbell Co., Va.), who lost his life, by the accidental discharge of a gun, from his own hand, on the 31st of October, 1856.]

Oh, laughing sunshine, shedding light
   O'er mountain, stream, and lea,
Why bring'st thou not a ray of joy
   To cheer my home, and me ;—
Alas ! in thy glad beams I trace
One vision fair,—an angel face.

In all bright things that speak to us
   Of innocence and mirth ;
The glittering star, the murmuring rill,
   The frail, young flowers of earth,—
In all I trace in lines of joy
The features of my buried boy.

And in each sighing tone that comes
　On wintry breezes borne ;
Whether from Nature's haunts bereft
　Or firesides drear and lone ;
A whispering voice in accents wild
Still speaks of my departed child.

Lost one !—thy smile returns again
　In Sunlight, Star,'and Flower,
But oh, a darker vision haunts
　This lonely musing hour ;
Methinks I see the current warm
Which stained thy stricken youthful form.

Oh, Memory ! thou canst paint for us
　No mournful portrait fair,
Of features paled by slow disease,
　Or wasting lines of care ;—
Love ne'er was privileged to keep
A " last watch" o'er *his* fevered sleep.

Gone from us ! wert thou tired of life
   Sweet Boy, that thine own hand
Should snap the subtle cord, and stay
   The swiftly flowing sand ;—
Was there no charm in home and hearth
To bind thee, for awhile, to Earth ?

Age pleads full oft for length of years,
   And pleads as oft in vain ;
Care, too, world-weary, murmurs, yet
   Would run the race again,—
And must thou quit the shores of Time
Ere Life had passed its flowery prime ?

Sweet Boy, had crime its guilty blight
   Thrown o'er thy heart a shade,
And thou hadst ended thus the woes
   Sin's blasting touch had made,—
Ah, then, I might have borne to see
The warm, fresh life-blood mantle thee.

Or, if Disease, with conquering strength,
   Had breathed upon thy brow,
And restless hours of anguish paled
   Thy young check's fervent glow;—
I might have closed the beaming eye,
And meekly bowed to see thee die.

But in my heart a vision dwells,
   A dark scene, strange and wild;
Yet as I gaze, Heaven's mystic light
   Surrounds my phantom child;—
And radiant forms of beauty glide
About thee, sinless Suicide!

I see thee, as on that bright morn,
   When, full of hope and joy,
Thou, like a warbling bird, went forth
   To come not back, my boy;
With gun in hand, and merry heart,
Sure thou must try the Huntsman's art.

And soon the sunlit rocks and hills
   Re-echoed with the sound,
Thy watchful, eager eye, methought
   Some luckless prize had found,—
But oh, too soon the echo came,—
A wild shriek coupled with thy name.

And then, to our half palsied arms
   Thy bleeding form was given;
The fatal ball had reached thy heart,
   Life's golden chords were riven;
We prayed, begged, wept, in anguish wild,
That Death would yield our guiltless child.

But all in vain,—no tears could heal
   The dark wound in thy side;
The crimson life-drops, fresh and warm,
   Still flowed—a streaming tide;
And when upon thy face so fair
We gazed, no answering smile was there.

Pale, cold and still—thy boyish face
　Ne'er looked more sweetly fair,
Than when Death's silent Angel left
　His frozen impress there,—
It seemed as though some Cherub bright
Had clothed each lineament in light.

My boy,—Spring's balmy touch may wake
　All other gladsome things;
The birds, the warbling birds may come,
　With sunshine on their wings,
But oh, their sweetest songs will be
But mournful requiems for thee.

And on each verdant hillside fair
　Earth's dewy flowers may spring,
And there the Butterfly may float
　Its rainbow-tinted wing,
But Summer-flowers will only wave
Their fragrant incense o'er thy grave.

And yet, I would not call thee back
　　To tread Life's path with me ;
I only ask, my angel boy,
　　That I may go to thee,
When Time's resistless cares are o'er,
And pain shall grieve the heart no more.

Child of my love, awhile farewell,
　　I feel thy presence nigh ;
Chiding each wayward, murmuring thought,
　　Each vain rebellious sigh,—
Then let my meek submission tell
His praise, who " *doeth all things well.*"

TO A WITHERING ROSE,

I HAD NURSED IN MY CHAMBER.

Alas! thou art fading, my beautiful flower!

To honor no more either garden or bower,—

Though Spring with its glories may come and restore

All its beauteous gifts to the glad earth once more;

Though Morn, fresh and balmy, may gather and
shed

Cool dews on thy gentle and languishing head;

Though Evening's soft breeze may still kiss thee
and sigh,

As in low fitful murmurs it passes thee by:

Not Morn's dewy fragrance nor Evening's pale light,

Can give back thy freshness or save thee from blight;

Yet I love thee the more, for in moments of sadness,

Sweet Rose, thou hast wakened my spirit to gladness;

19*

And now I will press thy frail stem to my heart,
And there let thy beauty and fragrance depart.
Ah, well I remember, pale, perishing flower!
The Morn when I pluck'd thee from Flora's gay
    bower;
Thy leaves were all laden with zephyrs and dew,
While the Sun o'er thy beauty a radiance threw;
And sure from the deference shown thee, I ween,
Thou wert of that bower the pride and the Queen.
By thy side the young hyacinths modestly grew,—
At thy feet were the violets, glistening with dew;
All around the young flowers peep'd forth to the
    light,
While the birds gaily carolled their song of delight.
How changed now the scene : surly Winter has come,
And invaded with boldness my own little room;
Even thou, the sweet gem that I've cherished so
    much,
Art yielding thy bloom to his cold, freezing touch.
What lesson, ah, what wouldst thou teach me, my
    flower,
By the pale, yellow hue that spreads o'er thee this
    hour?

Must I learn from thy gentle and lovely decay,
That the bright things of Earth are all passing
    away?
Then long shall I bless thee, that thou dost impart
So faithful a truth to my thoughtless young heart.

A MORNING AT CLIFF COTTAGE.

ALL Nature wakes with that soft, peering light
Which bright'neth yonder Orient.   See the flowers,
With what new joy they lift their pearly cups
To drink the fallen dew, while each young leaf
Stirs with a new-born grace to the soft touch
Of the light zephyr, passing o'er its face.
I bless God for the flowers, the dewy flowers,—
Their fragrant breath wakes in my heart new hopes,
And when at early morn I rouse from sleep,
And leave the quiet stillness of my room
To watch their perfumed welcome to the day,—
Methinks I see in this, an emblem meet
Of that delight the spirit must enjoy
When first its clay-sealed eyes open to greet
The radiant light of Heaven.   Ah ! silently
Ye teach, but sweetly, voiceless flowers !   Ye speak

Like Angels, without words, but ye, like them,
Speak truthfully, and by your frailty teach
The young heart sober lessons. Deep within
Your fragrant bosoms lie mysterious truths,
If man would only heed them. Fresh and fair
Ye hang upon your stems this glowing morn,
The dew yet glittering like sparkling gems
Upon each petal, till the passing breeze
Shakes off the shining drops, and leaves each tint
Of rainbow beauty, brighter than before.
Alas! too soon beneath a noontide sun,
Your slender heads will droop, and when at eve,
I come again to seek your perfumed smile,
A faded hue will rest upon your leaves;
Your blush and dewy freshness, vanished, gone,
And in my pathway, I shall soon behold
A group of withered flow'rets, blighted, *dead*.
Ah, such is life, frail blossoms! Such the end
Of hopes that waked in childhood's golden morn
Promise of coming joys. They yielded then
Their fragrant freshness to the early dawn
Of our brief day; and when we go back now,

To seek them by the wayside of the Past,
We only see around us *faded flowers.*
Yet why pause now, at this delicious hour,
To muse upon the sober truths of life ?
Enough to know, that Nature hath put on
Her robe of fairest loveliness to-day ;
That round me breathe her richest harmonies
Of thankfulness and joy.   Summer birds
Fly near, on gladsome wing, from tree to tree,
And from their warbling throats gush forth sweet
      notes
Of welcome to the morn.

         And e'en the vine
Of the Clematis, which above me climbs
Its tendrils sweet, hath oped its starry eyes,
To share the morning's favor with the Rose,
While 'neath the craggy cliff that skirts our home,
The murmuring "Hawksbill" sings itself along—
Dashing its sportive ripples to the light,
Or hiding 'mid the shades of forests dim
Its tuneful flow.   And, now afar I see,

Above yon mountain's brow the dazzling Sun,
Rising in glorious majesty, to give
New radiance to the scene.   His glowing face
Bathes hill and field, and flowing stream in light,
And 'neath the bright effulgence of his smile,
Earth seems a garden spot of Eden bloom.
Oh, God! my heart is full of gushing praise;
I bless thee for the Morn, and I would fain˙
Bless thee, kind Father, too, for the deep joy
Its freshness gives.   I would lift up my voice
Amid this din of Nature's melodies,
And say, with Bird, and Stream, and Flower,
I thank Thee, Great Creator, that I live.

WRITTEN FOR A MOTHER,

IN HER SON'S BIBLE, ON HIS LEAVING HOME FOR COLLEGE.

"My son, if sinners entice thee, consent thou not."
PROV. 1 : 10.

THE time has come, when thou must go
    Forth from thy mother's side ;
The world, its dangers and its snares,
    Now opens for thee wide.

Thou'lt miss her guiding hand, my boy,
    Her love's fond watch o'er thee,
Yet may this Book, her parting gift,
    Thy guide and counsel be.

When sin allures with siren tongue,
    And tempts thy feet to stray,

Let this bright way-mark point thee, then,
　To Christ, the Living Way.

When proud Ambition speeds thee on
　To glory and to fame,
Seek first God's kingdom,—love thou best
　A Christian's holy name.

When Hope's glad rainbow shines above,
　And all seems well with thee,
Prove thine own heart, and let this book
　That heart's pure standard be.

Dark days will come—the brightest sky
　Must sometimes be o'ercast,
Search then thy Bible, trust in God,
　Be faithful to the last.

AH, I FELT I WAS FORGOTTEN!

Ah, I felt I was forgotten,
　　I knew it by the spell
Of loneliness, and dark despair,
　　Which on my spirit fell.
It haunted me in Pleasure's halls
　　When all around were gay,
It came when joyous mirth and glee
　　Held everywhere their sway.

I could not smile when others smiled,
　　In vain they sought to chide,—
Pale Memory, a spectre, stood
　　Forever at my side.
And pointing with her finger wan,
　　To pictures of the past,
She shut from out my tearful heart
　　Fond hopes, too bright to last.

She bade me turn to bygone years,
   When I was all to thee;
When gushing from thy heart, there flowed
   A fount of love for me.
Of late, a fairer brow hath charmed
   That fickle heart of thine,
A siren-voice hath lured, and won
   The heart that once was mine.

What bitter tears these eyes have wept,
   I may not pause to tell;
Suffice, the pang is over now,
   I too can say farewell.
And I can backward gaze, nor feel
   One single fond regret,
I can *forgive*, too, thy false part,
   Do aught, but *not forget*.

A LITTLE HINT TO LITTLE BEAUX.

I'LL tell you lads, what sort of lass
  To fancy for a wife;
And by the way, no other kind
  Should 'harness *me* for life.'

I'd have her *be* a child, I mean
  In childhood so at least,
Not 'partying' when she should be at
  A bread-and-butter feast.

Not sporting hoops and crinoline,
  Or dress of silken goods,
When she might look so sweeter far
  In calico and hoods.

Not gazing absently in church,
　To where the 'buttons' flash ;
Not on the street, or anywhere,
　Seeking to '*cut a dash*.'

Not manifesting at her home
　A stubborn will, or strife ;
For if she's not obedient there,
　She'll not be so '*for life*.'

I'd choose a modest little girl,
　A girl with girlish ways ;
Retiring, gentle,—one whom none
　Could mention but to praise.

I'd watch her conduct everywhere ;
　From church, if it occurred,
I'd ask her what the text was—just
　To see if she had heard.

And on the street, I'd notice if—
　With silly, smirking air,

To every boy she chanced to meet,
  She nodded here and there.

And at her home, I'd look to see
  Each act with kindness rife,
A kind, good daughter's very apt
  To make a kind, good wife.

I'd mark her in the fireside group,
  To see a noble heart
Display itself, in things that bear
  Upon a sister's part.

And when the kitten from the hearth
  Come purring to her lap,
I'd notice if her welcome were
  A kind stroke, or—a slap.

And when I found one good and true
  As I would have her be,
When we were 'grown folks' I would ask
  Her then to marry me.

I tell you, boys, such is the girl
   To fancy for a wife;
And were I you, no other kind
   Should 'harness *me* for life.'

TO AN ONLY SISTER.

'Tis night, sweet sister, and the stars
    Are trembling in the sky,—
Brightly as when we watched their light
    In other years gone by.
The moon hath climbed the distant hill
    And decks Heaven's starry dome,
As when her soft rays shone around
    Our own, sweet childhood-home.

The Whippoorwill has hushed his song,
    The dew is on the ground,—
The flowers have closed their fragrant cups,
    And all is still around.
What marvel then that Memory's flight
    Should wing its way to thee;
And to the only parent dear
    Now left to you and me!

Our Mother lies asleep, the grave
    Hath hid her from our view,
And Father's eye is growing dim,
    And we are now but two.
The youngest of our parted band
    Wanders, an angel bright,
Where streams of " living waters" glide
    Through radiant realms of light.

Mother and child, united, dwell
    In that blest home on high,
While we are left, that path to seek
    Which led them to the sky.
By all the love we lost in them,
    By his, whose parent-care
Still follows us, where'er we go,
    With blessings and with prayer,

Let's be, through life, devoted, true,
    Sustaining each the other,
Remembering always the wish
    Of our sweet angel Mother.

In childhood's bright and sunny hours,
　　When hushed to rosy rest—
Soothed by the same low "lullaby,"
　　Clasped to the same fond breast.

How oft, ere envied slumber chained
　　Our senses with its spell,
Did these sweet words fall on our ear:
　　" *Love one another well.*"
The lips that breathed them, now are mute,
　　Death's seal upon them laid;
Yet ne'er may their soft music-tones
　　From our remembrance fade.

But let our hearts the motto heed
　　Each "loving well" the other—
Remembering the last, fond wish,
　　Of our sweet, angel mother.
Good night, beloved—the moonbeams fall
　　Gently o'er hill and lea,
The while I breathe, to listening Heaven,
　　Love's fervent prayer for thee.

NEWSBOY'S CHRISTMAS ADDRESS.

SINCE our last year's Christmas greeting,
  Faithful friends, and patrons kind,
We have followed one, whose footprints
  Leave a mournful shade behind.
We have seen the bright Spring blossoms
  Blooming fair on hill and dell,
And we've heard the gentle Summer,
  Breathe her plaintive, low farewell.

Then we've watched the meek-eyed Autumn
  With her mystic face serene;
Mantling all this world of ours
  In a robe of rainbow sheen.
Next, with noiseless step advancing,
  Winter comes with chilling breath;
Clothing hill, and vale, and mountain,
  In the livery of Death.

See you not, a Phantom figure
　　Drawing near, with features pale,—
Hear you not a requiem swelling?
　　'Tis the Old Year's dying wail.
Hark! the Christmas bells are chiming
　　With his moan, and busy feet,
All unmindful of the spectre,
　　Glide along the crowded street.

Let *us* join the merry circle,
　　And be happy while we may;
'Tis the *idle* workman, only,
　　Who deserves no holyday.
Spare us then the Christmas trifle,
　　We have never claimed in vain;
And may Heaven, in countless blessings,
　　Give it back to you again.

ON REVISITING THE HOME OF MY CHILDHOOD.

My heart beats with a quickened pulse. Behold,
The tide of Time rolls back!—I tread once more
The hallowed footprints of my earlier years;
This is the threshold, this the open door,
Through which my eager steps have entered in,
How oft before!

    Here, was my Mother's room ;
Aye, it was here she gave me birth, and here
These lips received her dying, farewell kiss.
A baby-sister lay, that dreary morn,
Upon her wasted breast,—now, both are gone.
* * * * * * * *
From this low window, I have often watched
The thick, fast falling of the summer rain,—

Fears for the birds, whose songs, the storm had
    hushed,
Haunting my childish breast. I little dreamed
That after years would shed upon my heart
Cold, pelting showers; that would drive Hope and
    Joy,
Like frightened birds, to fold their timid wings
'Neath the o'erdarkened sky. My heart looks up
And thanks thee, Father, that thou minglest thus
Thorns with the flowers about Life's pathway
    strewn.
These would but bind us *here;* those point us where
No clouds shut out Heaven's sunshine from the
    soul.
Oh, how "old times" come back!—This mansion
    old,
With its dim halls, and silent chambers lone,
Tells a sweet tale of childhood happiness.
There was a time, when nook and corner rang
With the glad shout of merry voices. Aye,
'Twas here I passed the joyous, fleeting hours
Of life's glad Springtime,—now, each way I turn

Some old familiar haunt calls up the Past.
My Grandmother's room! I well remember
How, when Mother died, we shared it with her,—
Sisters two, I and our little cousins,
A helpless band, to whom she did become
The second mother. Ah, long years have passed
Since on her gentle form we looked our last.
You crumbling porch led to the parlor, where,
With songs and music, passed the evening hours.
Even now I see the quaint old pictures
Hanging 'gainst the walls,—my father's portrait,
Picturing him in all the pride of manhood.
This was the dining-room; just on that spot
Stood the old sideboard; there the little stand
On which the Bible rested; here the desk
And time-worn bookcase,—relics quaint and old.
I shut mine eyes, and see the table spread,—
I almost hear the laughing jest go round,
From loving lips, now voiceless. Aye, the Dead,
Come back to-day, and seem to fill once more,
Their old accustomed places. Absent ones
Long parted meet—but mournful thoughts shut out

The cherished vision, and I look to see
Only the dreary change which time hath wrought.
There is the tree beneath whose leafy shade
We oft *"kept house"* in Summer's noontide hours,
Wooing the'birds and butterflies for guests,
And chiding them that they did seem to scorn
Our mimic hospitality.

That path
Led to the schoolhouse, where we first did learn
To *welcome* *" rainy days;"* and where, full oft,
The forfeit of a playtime had to pay
For playing truant at the grapevine swing.
Oh, halcyon days of sunshine and of joy!—
There is the garden with its rustic gate
Crowned with gay trumpet flowers; how oft before
I've seen it thus, in other years gone by,
Only more beautiful beneath the light
Which childhood's gaze is wont to shed on all
Around, above, about us.   Shrub and vine,
The very rose I planted bloomed more fair,
When I, a glad child, watched each mystic growth,
And proudly hailed each new development.

That beaten road led to Mount Olivet,—
The country Church whose Summer Sabbath-school
I can recall as 'twere but yesterday.
Yon shady grove, parting the meadow green,
Circles the spring, the bright, clear, gushing spring,
Whose crystal depths mirrored each waving bough
That hung above it.   'Twas a favorite spot
Whereby to loiter when we came from school,—
Tired out with rules, "hard lessons," and dull books.
I can remember how, in Summer time,
We made our play-house here, on holidays,—
Launching our mimic boats made up of leaves
And hickory-nut shells, on the eddying stream,
Whose gurgling fountain was that woodland spring.
And then 'twas sweet to come at sultry noon,
And sit beneath those tall, proud forest trees,
Whose twining arms stretched out protectingly
Above our heads.   Ah, we were careless then,
And young, and free, *a little band of six*,—
All motherless.   Grief could not long have sway
O'er hearts so blest with love's kind sympathies.
We did not know that Death would lay his hand

On others of our household, and that Time
Would rob us of this home we loved so well,—
That stranger hands would tend the flowers we
    reared,
And write strange records on familiar things.
Lo! where yon sunlight falls so tenderly
Upon a hillside fair, are the lone graves
Of our departed ones. There rest our Dead;
There sleeps my mother close beside her own,
Who, in my childhood, held her place to me.
Peace to their ashes, peace, beloved Dead!
To you may come no more sunshine or storm;
Yet well I know, that He whose kind eye marks
The sparrow's fall, will guard your sleeping dust,
Till He shall bid it rise. Oh, may He then
Unite again, each precious, parted link
Of our glad household chain, and may we dwell
Together in that changeless clime above,
Where Death comes never more, and where no tears
Fall from fond eyes o'er ruins Time hath made.
The evening shadows fall, how soft and still,
Upon this hallowed scene,—the air is hushed,

The mellow rays of the declining sun
Shed a mild radiance on each object round,—
Nature breathes in concord with my spirit,—
Wood, rock, and hill, echo my parting words.
Graves of my Dead! Home of my heart! farewell.

TO BLANCHE.

LITTLE one, with pensive eye,
Soft and blue as yonder sky;
Lip as pure as Summer flower,
Wet with dew at morning hour;
Form of fair and fragile mould,
Heart where love can ne'er grow cold;
Voice as sweet as cooing dove
When it mourns its absent love;
In thy mirth, so blithe and free,
What is Life, sweet one, to thee?

Such the language of thy face,
So much sadness, so much grace;
Such thy noiseless step, as light
As the poet's dreams at night;

Such the soft, appealing tone,
Of thy voice, like music's own,
That I've thought there ne'er should dwell
In thy heart one shadowy spell;
That all joy and peace should be
Mingled in Life's cup for thee.

May it prove that years will shed
Blessings on thy gentle head;
Faith a sacred halo fling,
Radiant as the dawn of Spring;
Hope, forever near thy side,
Linger still an Angel guide;
Love lend ever her soft light
To direct thy steps aright,
And to thy young heart be given
Peace and happiness from Heaven.

STEWART HOLLAND,

THE HERO-VICTIM OF THE LOST "ARCTIC."

"He could not be induced to leave the ship; his post was at the gun, firing signals; he kept firing the gun till the vessel sunk; we saw him in the very act of firing as the vessel disappeared below the waters."

A REQUIEM for thee, oh, true and brave!
Whose winding-sheet is the Atlantic wave;
No braver heart e'er sunk 'neath Ocean's surge,—
Ill-fated Holland! billows moan thy dirge.

And ah! how many fond eyes vainly weep,
As, gazing o'er the trackless, foaming deep,
A voice comes to them with the Sea's sad moan,
That tells of thee, their loved, brave, perished one!

True to thy trust, and to thine honor true,—
Alone in all that panic-stricken crew;

No fears disarmed, nor did thy bosom quail,
Though stout hearts faltered, and stern lips grew
   pale.

Rough, hardy seamen rushed by thee on deck,
Each struggling to escape the fearful wreck;
Men, women, children, frantic with despair,
Pierced with their shrieking tones the misty air.

And high above, the startled sea-bird soared,
While close beneath thee, angry billows roared;
Yet, at thy post, unflinching to the last,
Thou heed'st not then the danger threatening fast.

But all undaunted, self-forgetting, brave,
Thou stood'st unmoved,—thy life to duty gave;
Nor ceased to fire thy mournful signal-gun,
'Till Death pronounced thy martyr-duty done.

Down went the noble ship, till Ocean's roar
Mingled with cries of human woe no more;
Manhood and Beauty, Love and Hope and Pride,
All sunk beneath the foaming, billowy tide.

Firm on the deck, deserted, thou didst stand,
The last of that ill-fated, hapless band ;
One signal more,—then down to Ocean's caves,
As that last sound dies o'er the engulfing waves.

What yearning thoughts were thine, in that dark
    hour,
No tongue may tell,—yet trusting to that Power,
Whose voice the winds and restless waves obeyed,
We know His arm thy dauntless spirit stayed.

And if, in Memory's vista, then arose
Faces and forms beloved, whose life's repose
Linked with thy love, henceforth must broken be,
He whispered softly, "Leave them all to me."

Ah! nobly hast thou yielded thy young life,
With all high purposes and proud aims rife ;
Martyr to Duty!—thou hast given to Fame
The long, sweet echo of a hero's name.

A LITTLE HINT TO LITTLE BELLES.

And now I'll tell you, little girls,
  What sort of boy to choose,—
For husbands are like lotteries,
  You win a prize or lose.

I'd have him be a boy—at least
  Till far down in his "teens;"
Not squandering in idle trash,
  His little surplus means.

Not boasting of his "fast" exploits,
  To prove himself a man;
Not turning out a scant mustache,
  To show you that he can.

Not bragging that he goes to church,
   Only to see who's there,
And that in sermons *he* could have
   No interest or share.

Not jeering what the preacher says,
   As foolish "stuff" and vain,
Avowing that he'd never let
   Such "*talk*" disturb his brain.

Not sauntering along the street,
   With stately step and air,
As though for "*small things*"—Books or
     Work—
   He had no *taste* to spare.

Not *every lassie's lad* he meets—
   No service be refused,
Except when "*Sister*" asks his aid,
   And then he'd "*be excused.*"

Not twirling a shillaly "nice,"
   Within a nicer hand,

While talking of his parents, as
  " Old woman" and " old man."

Not "dropping in" at bar-room haunts,
  To get—*a good cigar* (*!*)
When well he knows a Father's eye
  Would frown to see him there.

Not interspersing idle talk
  With "*small oaths*" here and there,
Regardless that a Mother's heart
  Would ache to hear him swear.

Not fearing lest he should be thought
  Unmanly, foolish, weak,
If from temptation's snare he'd turn
  Some loftier aim to seek.

I'd choose a boy that's bold and brave—
  Not impudent or fast,
But one who'd *dare to do the right*,
  Undaunted to the last.

I'd have him be industrious,
  And persevering, too—
Doing with willing hand and heart,
  Whate'er he had to do.

I'd watch him closely on the street,
  To see him shun the place,
Where, 'neath a Father's frowning eye,
  He'd blush to show his face.

I'd note him in the house of God,
  And at the hour of prayer,
To see a close, attentive ear,
  And reverential air.

I'd mark his conduct well abroad,
  And at his fireside, too,—
A "*mother's son*" is apt to make
  A husband kind and true.

I'd notice when his humble dog
  Ventured his hand to lick,

Whether his welcome impulse were
  A "soft pat" or *a kick*.

Or when I'd satisfy myself,
  If he were kind or cross,
I'd only wait some careless time,
  To watch him with his horse.

If he were gentle, brave, and good,
  As noble boys should be,
I'd wait till we were grown,—then let
  Him whisper love to me.

For I should feel that I had found
  A heart both true and warm,
On which my own might safely lean,
  Through sunshine and through storm.

So, if my parents both agreed
  To let me be his wife,
I'd tell him so, and joining hands,
  We'd settle down "for life."

I tell you, girls, all jest aside,
  Such is the boy to choose;
For husbands are like lotteries,—
  You win a prize, or lose.

A SISTER'S FAREWELL.

How shall we give thee up,
　Brother, so dear?
Glad is the household band
　While thou art here.
Changed, changed will be the hearth,
　Dreary and lone,
Vanished our life's delight,
　When thou art gone.
How shall we give thee up,
　Noblest and best?
Happy have been the hearts
　Thy smile hath blest.
Brightly our childhood passed,
　Thy love its star;
Memory now sees its light
　Shining afar.

Gladly the days flew by,
    Thou at my side,
Pleasure and mirthfulness
    On thee relied.
Oft by the river's brink
    Culled we the flowers,
Wreathed them in garlands gay
    For Summer hours.
Then tired of passive sports,
    Chased we the bee,
I, full of childish trust,
    Following thee.
Ah! those were joyous times;
    Would, but how vain,
Childhood's unclouded days
    Might come again.
Would that its faith and hope
    Time might restore;
But vainly said, those joys
    Come back no more.
Gone is life's sweet spring-time,
    Faded its bloom,

O'er the heart's cherished hopes
   Rests autumn's gloom.
Now the dark hour has come
   When thou must roam—
Life's slippery path untried,
   Far from thy home.
All the deep yearning love,
   Trusting and tried,
Which in our childhood years,
   Clung to thy side,
Follow thee, brother dear,
   .From our lone hearth,
Where'er thy steps may stray
   O'er the broad earth.
Oh, may Heaven's blessing rest
   On thee through life—
Shield thee in time of need,
   Danger and strife.
May God his grace bestow,
   Make thee his care;
This be my last farewell,
   This my last prayer.

FLOWERS

FROM THE CONVENT OF MT. DE SALES, NEAR
BALTIMORE.

PRESENTED BY "SISTER CECILIA."

Ye wert born afar from the haunts of men,
   In the shades of the perfumed bowers;
Ye wert given to me by a gentle hand,
   With a kindliest smile, fair flowers.
And though passed long since is your fragrant
      breath,
   And the light of your blooming hours,
Yet I love, ah! well, the sweet memories linked
   With your brief, fleeting lives, pale flowers.
Ye wert watched, aye long, by an eye as bright
   As the stars that look down at even;
And your smiles did gladden a heart as pure
   As the Seraphs who smile in Heaven.

How well I remember that sweet retreat,
  Her home—in its calm seclusion,
Like an isle of beauty, where fairies dwell,
  Shut out from mortal obtrusion.
'Tis a woodland wild, where the squirrel's chirp,
  And the hum of the mountain bee,
Blend in chorus glad with the red bird's note,
  And the oriole's, so blithe and free.
'Tis a hillside fair, from whose verdant crest
  Rose the Convent spire,—ah, well
I recall, e'en now, how it pointed then
  To that home, where the sinless dwell.
And I thought of one, in her girlhood's bloom,
  More fair than these flowers so cherished,
Whose bright cheek grew pale 'neath my anxious
    gaze,
  Whose form from my side had perished.
I murmured her name—the echo which came
  Was soft as the whispers of even,
And when it was lost to my ear, I gazed—
  The spire—still—still pointed to Heaven!

How sadly I mused, as I clasped her hand,
  Who had guided us both in youth—
A "Sister" in name to me and to mine,
  She was "Mother" indeed and in truth.
Around me were faces and forms beloved,
  In the bright days of "Auld Lang Syne,"
When my life was new and my heart was young,
  And the day-dreams of youth were mine,
And near me were voices whose sweet, low tones,
  Led my spirit rejoicing back,
With its burden of years, to roam again
  O'er my lost childhood's shining track.
I lingered long, and on Memory's wall
  Hangs the picture I saw that day,
Of the woodland wild, with its Convent spire,
  And, distant, the beautiful Bay.
Can I ever forget it?—pure and sweet
  As the odor of Southern gales,
Is the dream I hold in my heart of hearts,
  Of that visit to Mt. de Sales.
In those cloistered halls there are forms as bright
  As a painter might love to trace—

Of innocent Childhood with laughing brow,

    And of Beauty, with half-veiled face.

As I stood mid that black-veiled group, each smile

    Woke the past, with its mystical train

Of my school-day joys, with their roseate hues—

    Lost blessings, which come not again.

While we strolled through those stately halls, they

        rang

    With the echoes of voices clear,

And the merry sound waked a slumbering chord,

    As I, musingly, paused to hear.

'Twas the laughing shout of a happy band,

    At their play on the green below—

Meek innocence smiled in each fair young face,

    Joy beamed from each beautiful brow;

Then my own glad school-days came back to me,

    And I thought of my playmates fair,—

Some had passed, long since, to the Silent Land,

    Some were living,—I knew not where.

And a murmured prayer went up from my heart

    To Our Father who reigneth above,

That when Death shall have gathered every one,

  . We may meet in His Home of Love!

On we passed, through corridors, rich and grand,

  With their frescoes and pictured walls,—

Art, Industry, Learning, and Genius too,

  Find a home in these cloistered halls.

The clock told the fast-fleeting hours,—too soon

  Came the moment to say farewell,—

Still I paused,—my heart beat faster the while,

  As we entered our loved one's cell.

'Twas a neat, small room, where we paused before

  A shrine of the Virgin and Child,—

The Babe looking up in the meek, bowed face

  Of the Mother, so pure and mild.

At the feet of the Virgin stood a vase,

  Newly filled from the garden bowers,

And from out that vase, the dear hand I held,

  Culled, and gave me these pale sweet flowers.

With a smile she added, " *They'll tell of us,*"

  And my heart gave its answer true,

As in silence I clasped each friendly hand,

  And in silence, wept an adieu!

Oh ! voiceless flowers, ye are faded now !
   Yet sweet as the echoes of even
Is the tale ye tell of that woodland wild,
   With its spire that pointed to Heaven.
And though distant far is that sunny spot,
   More pure than the soft Southern gales,
Is the dream I hold in my heart of hearts,
   Of that visit to Mt. De Sales.
Long, long may the picture my spirit cheer,
   With its rainbow tints, lovely and bright,
Till Death to my soul fairer visions unfold
   In the radiant regions of Light.

MY LITTLE STAR.

I've watched a Star, dear one, since last we parted,
 A solitary star which shines above,
As though 'twould lure me, by its strange pure
 brightness,
 To dream, once more, of happiness and love.

A little trembling star, it shines at even,
 So pure, so holy, too, its soft rays are,—
I almost question if some Angel spirit
 Does not bend o'er me from that little star.

At twilight, when my saddened heart is lonely,
 That star looks calmly down as though to cheer
My weary bosom, when dim spectres only
 And shadows of the Past are gliding near.

Each dewy evening as I gaze upon it,
    So mild, so heavenly, as it shines afar,
I, musing, wonder if its soft light reacheth
    Beyond those mountain summits where you are.

I wonder, too, whether your eyes behold it,
    The while I gaze upon its mystic light,—
If so, then tell me, does it charm your spirit
    By its soft rays, so beautiful and bright?

A cloud passed o'er my little star this evening,
    A cold, dark cloud, so cold, it made me weep;
Yet still I mused, mine eyes still upward gazing
    Through blinding tears, their silent watch to
        keep.

And when I bowed me down in prayerful sorrow,
    A sudden calmness swept my spirit o'er,—
I gazed again, and lo! the cloud had vanished,—
    My little star shone brighter than before.

Didst view it thus, beloved, and didst thou question
    The direful omen when the cloud appeared?

23*

And did thy soul, like mine, bow down in sorrow?
   And was thy heart's deep fountain strangely
     stirred?

And didst thou welcome, too, the star's returning,
   When pure, and beautiful, and calm, and bright,
It shone again, more radiant still, still soothing
   Our fevered senses by its mystic light?

Thus may Life's path for thee, dear one, be lighted
   By Hope's glad ray which dawneth from above,
And may each transient cloud which passes o'er it
   But add new radiance to thy Star of Love.

This silent prayer my fond lips utter nightly,
   As through the shadows dim and mists of even,
My little Star looks down and seems to whisper
   Of Peace, and Happiness, and Love, in Heaven.

LIGHT IN DARKNESS.

A FRAGMENT.

THIS world is not all darkness,—forms of light
Float ever round us in the thickest night;
Kind, minst'ring spirits pass us to and fro
With ready greeting in this vale of woe.
And on us from their radiant home, the skies,
Bright, guardian angels look with tender eyes,—
Or, sent to earth upon some high behests,
They leave their starry sphere to be our guests.
And hov'ring 'round us on their viewless wings,
They cheer the heart with silent whisperings
Of endless joy and peaceful rest above,
Where in God's presence all is light and love;
Where life's dull cares and mocking fears all o'er,
Sorrow shall pain the timid heart no more.

Where clouds no longer o'er our footsteps rise
To hide the light that on our pathway lies.
Where Hope's glad song may greet th' Eternal ear,
And Faith is lost in vision bright and clear.
Where from the heart there comes no grieving
    moan
For friendship lost, no quenchless murmuring tone
Of silent suffering it is pressed to bear,
With no kind bosom in its grief to share.
Look up, sad spirit, o'er yon azure dome
Is thy inheritance, that blessèd home
Whose portals open for the faithful heart,
Subdued and chastened by affliction's smart.
Our Father offers it; can *He* deceive?
The sole condition is "*repent, believe.*"
Oh, rouse thee, heart! rush to thy Master's fight;
His yoke is easy and his burden light;
Shake off Sin's rankling fetter—strength is *His*
Whose faithful service perfect freedom is.
His eye will watch, His arm protect thee here
From lurking foes and dangers threat'ning near.

His love will guide thee through that vale of gloom
Which leads to fields of fresh, immortal bloom;
Where thou mayst wander by those crystal streams,
On whose clear depths the Sun of Glory beams.
In that bright land no cherished flow'rets lie
Fresh in our pathway, then bow down and die.
No gentle spirits,—formed to bless and cheer
Our yearning bosoms while we linger here,—
Stay with us only till their love hath made
The light that round our weary footsteps played;
Then leaving us, of banished joy no trace,
Say, " *Fare-thee well*," and quit our fond embrace.
In that sweet, heavenly clime, no tears are shed
In helpless anguish o'er the loved and dead;
No mem'ries haunt us of fond eyes that shone
On us in love, their light now quenched and gone,—
Eyes that looked on us with sad lustre bright,
Then meekly closed in Death's dim, starless night.
No lips delight us with fond tones awhile,
Then on our darken'd pathway cease to smile.
No voice comes to us in low tones and clear,
Mocking with its sweet melody, the ear—

Telling of lips whose whispers hushed and gone
Once gladdened us like music's softest tone.
No silent, secret woe is ours to bear;
No tearful eyes, no broken hearts are there.
But lost in rapture, fill'd with boundless love,
The freed soul wanders in those realms above;
The praise of God, its endless theme and song,
While Seraphs the ecstatic notes prolong.
Heart, bear on bravely, to thyself be true;
Whate'er betide thee, keep thy goal in view;
Assured that for the chastened spirit given,
There yet remaineth a sweet rest in Heaven,
Where the swift, fleeting hours of Time shall be
Lost in the reck'ning of *Eternity*.

TO ISABEL.

WITH THE BRIDAL-GIFT OF A BIBLE.

Let others bring their gifts to thee,
   Of silver and of gold,—
Rare pearls from India's coral seas,
   Rich gems from Oceans old :
Mine be this Bible,—blessèd book,
   A friend, sincere and true,—
A beacon star, to light the way
   Thy footsteps should pursue.

Clasp it with fervor to thy heart
   Now, in thy bridal hours,
'Twill wake new joys within thy soul,
   And strew thy path with flowers.

Study its precepts—it will prove
 A guide, both safe and sure,
When earthly dangers threaten near,
 And earthly snares allure.

Hold it while living—search its truths,—
 Make sure its promise sweet.
" A light 'twill be unto thy path,
 A lamp unto thy feet ;"
Clasp it when dying, it will prove
 A talisman, pure and bright,—
To guide thee through Death's shadowy vale,
 Up—to the Land of Light.

MY MARY.

(A HUSBAND'S LAMENT.)

I KNEW that we must part—
 She often told me so,
But I did not know how hard
 'Twould be to let her go;
I knew not till it came
 How hard the stroke must be
Which made my joy, a dream—
 My hope, a memory.

I watched her fading cheek,
 Slow step, and languid eye;
I prayed that she might live,
 I felt that she must die.

24

And when the moment came,
   An angel hushed her breath;
I said it must be sleep,
   They told me it was Death.

My eyes were blinded now,
   I nothing saw that day,
Till in a coffin dim
   Her slumbering face of clay,
Mute lips that would not speak,
   A placid forehead fair;
Closed eyes, a marble cheek,
   And stirless folds of hair.

Oh! God, if word of mine
   E'er pained that pulseless heart,
If e'er I caused a tear
   In that closed eye to start:
Let her pure spirit speak,
   And say I am forgiven,
Ere yet the "pearly gates"
   Have shut her in Thy Heaven.

No answering look or smile,
   Only a dreadful sound,
Which struck against my heart,
   When they screwed the black lid down.
I turned to go—but where?
   The waiting hearse is near,—
They've borne my Mary out,
   And I must follow her.

Beside an open grave
   They paused, and prayers were read;
Then busy hands threw in
   Dull clods upon the dead.
They piled the fresh, cold earth
   Above her silent breast;
Two heavy stones were laid,
   To mark her place of rest.

Their part was over now;
   They left me, one by one;
The sexton, with his spade,
   His weary task was done.

But I—where could I go?
   How turn me from that mound,
Where slept my gentle wife,
   My Mary, in the ground?

Oh! this is worse than death,
   To breathe, yet not to live;
To know that all the world
   Hath no more joy to give.
I'll go from place to place,
   Do aught the hours to vary;
But not on earth again
   Shall I behold my Mary.

A PLACE AT THY FEET, OH! MY SAVIOUR.

AIR—"*A place in thy memory, dearest.*"

A PLACE at Thy feet, oh! my Saviour,
  Is all that I claim,—
That in the Lamb's Book of remembrance
  Thou wilt write my name.
Let others seek fortune and pleasure,
  The world and its phantoms pursue,—
Thou only canst give lasting treasure,
  Immortal and true.

Remember me, Lord, as a sinner,
  Weak, erring, and blind;
No merit I bring as a passport
  Thy favor to find.

24*

No price can I offer for pardon,
  Thy grace must be freely supplied ;
A worm in Thy sight, poor and helpless,
  For such Thou hast died.

Remember Gethsemane's garden,
  Thine anguish and prayer ;
The sadness which bowed down Thy spirit
  In agony there.
Remember thy soul's desolation,
  Thy death upon Calvary ;
And, oh ! from that cross, bleeding Jesus,
  Turn thy dying eyes on me.

When shineth Hope's rainbow above me,
  And earth seems most fair ;
Dear Lord, in thy wisdom unerring,
  Still make me Thy care.
When the sunlight of Fortune is beaming
  In days of prosperity,
And the cup of my joy runneth over,
  Dear Jesus, remember me.

When the light o'er life's pathway is darkened
By sorrow and gloom,
And the flowers of Hope I have cherished
Lie stripped of their bloom ;—
When sickness and Death overtake me,
And Earth's mocking phantoms shall flee ;
As I walk through the Valley of Shadows,
Dear Saviour, remember me.

OLD WINTER HAS COME.

Old Winter has come again: harsh through the door
    The cold, chilling blasts creep in ;
The fast-falling snow-flakes are gathering without,
    The hickory blazing within.

Old Winter has come, aye, and we are all blest
    With plenty of warmth and of bread ;
While many a creature is braving the storm
    With no shelter to cover his head.

Old Winter has come, and the trees are all clad
    In their beautiful vestures of snow.
The dark, threatening storm-clouds are lowering
        above,
    The rivulets freezing below.

Old Winter has come, see, the snow-bird hops round
  And chirps for a spare little crumb,
While on, Master Harry still heedlessly sings
  The song of Bopeep and Tom Thumb.

Old Winter has come; the bold schoolboy cries out,
  "Old Winter's the season for me;"
And high in the air the bright snow-balls are
    hurled,
  With a halloo of innocent glee.

Old Winter has come; yes, but ah! not to all
  Does he bring with him laughter and mirth,—
E'en to-day there are little ones shivering around
  Full many a comfortless hearth.

Old Winter has come; then remember the poor,
  Relieve their sad wants whilst ye may,—
What ye have, what ye are, ye owe all to His love
  Who hath given and can take away.

OVER!

THE struggle is over—the agony past,
And the dear little sufferer is quiet at last;
Press down the fringed lids o'er those shadowless
    eyes
Where the spirit of beauty and holiness lies;

Then fold the soft hands on his innocent breast,
Nought now can disturb the sweet calm of his rest;
He has felt the last pang, he has yielded his
    breath,
And his sleep is the still, dreamless slumber of
    death.

Thank God, he is done now with sickness and pain,
Would I call his freed soul to its prison again—

Would I bar the glad things, the bright joys of
    Heaven,
From his spirit, whom Death to the angels hath
    given ?

Ah no, yet I bury in Earth's frozen breast
The hopes I have cherished as dearest and best;
To thy voiceless keeping, oh ! Grave, I impart
The joy of my being—the pearl of my heart.

One kiss on the marble cheek—baby, farewell !
Thy home now is where only blest ones may dwell.
Too bleak was our pathway, oh, sinless, for thee ;
Thy fetters are broken—bright seraph, thou'rt free.

We lay thy dear form in the grave, yet no gloom
Can reach thee, pale flower, cut down in thy
    bloom ;
In Heaven, where thou art now, bliss is thy part;
No blight shall fall on thee there, Bud of my heart.

A LITTLE BOY'S WISH AND RESO-
LUTION.

"I WANT my mamma!" said a beautiful boy,
  As the bright, early morn was breaking,—
He had opened his eyes, and no fresh, warm kiss
  Fell soft on his lips, at his waking.

"I want my mamma!" and his bright azure eyes,
  With fast-gathering tears were filling,
While his piteous tones swelled a father's heart
  With an anguish deep and thrilling.

And, lifting his little one on his knee,
  He smoothed back the golden tresses,
While only a sob from the motherless child,
  Could answer his fond caresses.

Then he told of a radiant clime above,
  Where tempest and storms come never,
To blight the immortal flowers that bloom
  On the banks of the crystal river.

And he said, " In that region of fadeless bloom,
  Is the friend to your infancy given ;
Last night, while you slept, lo ! an angel came,
  And carried your mother to Heaven.

" Oft, oft in that beautiful land, my child,
  Where sorrow and death come never,
Young children and mothers, long parted, meet,
  With no more partings forever."

The boy, looking up with a wondering gaze,
  His eye kindling bright at the story,
Said, "I wish the good Angel who took my mamma,
  Would come back and take me to glory."

" Then be a good boy," the sad father replied,
  " Let nought her pure influence smother ;

25

And in God's own time the good Angel will come,
And carry you home to your mother."

Bounding off with a heart full of childish delight,
His bosom relieved of its sorrow,—
" *I'll make haste to be good, Pa,*" the innocent said,
"*And then maybe he'll take me to-morrow.*"

AN EVENING AT CLIFF COTTAGE.

'Tis moonlight on the mountains; and around
A brooding stillness, save the night-wind's tone,
Wooing sweet rest amid the folded flowers,
Or mingling with the Whip-poor-will's sad song,
To swell the fading echoes that resound
So softly from the parting melodies
Of day.   It is the hour when holy truths
Press deeply on the heart,—the boundless might
And majesty of God!   His voice proclaimed
"Let there be light!"   And lo, the earth was
        bathed
In radiance; Nature smiled, and warbling throats
Swelled with a morning pæan.   Now He bids
The dazzling sun withdraw, and moonlight falls
Gently on vale and mountain.   Oh, how sweet

Its message to the spirit: " *God is love !*"
The zephyrs bear it in their whispering tones,
As with a murmuring sigh they breathe " Good
    night,"
And sleep among the blossoms.   It is read
Upon each tiny leaflet, and the flowers
Proclaim it from their perfumed cells, e'en now,
As dreamily they hang, all wet with dew,
Yielding their farewell fragrance to the night.
Aye, it is heard, too, in the lulling flow
Of our own streamlet, as it winds around
The rugged cliff, telling of Him who made
Each trembling star that's mirrored in its face.
Hush, beating heart, be still !   I fain would catch
Each murmur of its melody.   I feel
An angel presence hovering 'mid this scene,
And musing thought, guided by its sweet spell,
Looks upward to the Infinite.   Oh, Thou,
Beneath whose watchful eye this great world
    sleeps ;
Under whose parent care the tiniest bird
May fold its wing in peace ; whose love extends

E'en to the smallest butterfly that plays
All day with sunbeams in the lily's cup;
Teach me to live, that when Death's shadows fall
Around me at life's evening, hope may smile
Like moonlight on my heart, and whisper low
Its message to my spirit: *"God is love!"*

25*

NOT AGAIN.

Not again, lady fair;
  Never, ah! never;
Thou who didst sport the chain,
  Rent it forever.

Gone is the spirit's trust,
  Gone, and forever;
Thou canst not call it back,
  Charming deceiver.

Once it were pain to part,—
  Then I believed thee;
Now I can bear the smart,—
  Thou hast deceived me.

A SABBATH IN MAY.

How peacefully Heaven's light upon thee dawns,
Sweet day of rest. A mellow radiance
Falls from bright skies o'er all this blooming earth,
And softly to the ear comes the slow chime
Of distant Sabbath bells. The weary heart
Throws off its weight of earthly cares, calls back
Its scattered thoughts the while, and yields itself
To its immortal promptings. Prayer now parts
The faithful Christian's lip, and the soft air
Bears to the sinner's heart, a sweet, low tone,
Which seems to say, "Repent." Not harshly falls
Upon his ear that mute, appealing voice,
As if th' avenging wrath of Heaven e'en now
Was ripening for him, if he longer grieved

God's long-forbearing Spirit,—but a low
Pleading tone, all rife with mournful music,
As if borne by Angel tongues from Calvary,
Aye, breathing of love, long-suffering love,
It steals upon his heart and wakes within
An answering chord of earnest penitence.
Anon, he wanders sadly forth, beneath
The azure arch of Heaven, and feels the touch
Of soothing summer warmth steal softly o'er
His weary temples.   It is God's light
That dawns so cheeringly upon him, 'tis
His atmosphere that feeds that principle
Of life within his veins.   It is His air
That plays about his forehead, and he hears
A mute reproach from Nature.   Gazing round,
Sees bird and bee, and blossom, busy all
In their own sphere of duty,—Man alone,
Of all created things, most favored, too,
Delinquent.   Timid flowers look meekly up
With their bright smiling eyes, and seem to say,
" We cheerfully fulfil our destiny,
We obey our glorious Maker's will,—

Why do not you, for whom Earth yields her gifts
Of fragrant bloom and beauty, and for whom
We smilingly discharge our mission pure,
Of summer joy and sunshine?"

LITTLE RANNIE.

INSCRIBED TO MR. AND MRS. WILLIAM R. BARBEE.

I HELD him in my arms, the while
    Death nearer drew each hour,
Until, at length, a blighting change
    Passed o'er the little flower.

He did not shrink, but unto me
    A long, fixed gaze was given,
And well I knew the pearly gates
    Now stood ajar in Heaven.

I clasped his hand, and closer drew
    The sweet face to my bosom,
But all the while Death waited near,
    To cull the dying blossom.

And when, at last, his icy breath
  Swept o'er the form so cherished,
A still, pale lip was all that told
  The little flower had perished.

A nestling Dove might so have died—
  Fearless, and tranquil-hearted;
As lilies droop, and violets fade,
  The baby-soul departed.

And when the spirit pure, had fled
  Back to our Father's keeping,
A smile lit up the pale, cold face,
  As of an Angel sleeping.

And soon we dressed him for the grave,
  And smoothed his shining tresses;
I knew the while, he did not *need*
  Our yearning fond caresses.

But yet my heart went out to you,
  Sad father, stricken mother,

And ah I felt how hard to yield
　Our dear ones to another.

We laid him in the coffin dim,—
　No ties of earth now bound him;
A spotless shrine of dust he lay,
　Spring's early flowers around him.

And now where hemlock branches wave
　O'er mountain-summits, keeping
A silent watch o'er lonely graves,
　.His baby-form is sleeping.

Look up, then, to our Father's House,
　With all your love immortal,—
Look up; behold, there waits for you
　An Angel at the portal.

SONG.

Air—"*I've Wandered by the Brookside.*"

AND must our spirits severed be,
  And must we say farewell,—
We who have nursed so tenderly
  The hopes we dared not tell.
Fast gushing tears are trembling now,
  In eyes that once were bright,
And hearts that bounded joyously,
  Are sunk in cheerless night.

How hard the fate that thus will break
  Hearts fondly pledged and true,
How sadly falls, from lips that love,
  That parting word, "Adieu!"
But, be it so, though never more
  On earth, Hope's light may shine,
There's comfort in the single thought,
  That still in Heaven thou'rt mine.

"ASHES OF ROSES."*

BRING hither snowy garlands fair,
   And wreathe them round her head,
Bring violets and lily-bells
   To crown the youthful Dead.

Ah! hither bring the "bridal wreath,"
   And place it on her brow,—
That brow, so warm beneath its folds,
   Alas! so frozen now.

Three fleeting months!—too soon, too soon,
   The joyous marriage bell
Is hushed,—a wail is on the air,
   A wail,—her funeral knell.

* On the death of Isabel, daughter of John O. L. Goggin—wife
of F. C. Hutter, of Lynchburg, Va.

Three months!—a brilliant festive scene,
   Mirth, wit, and laughter loud,—
To-day a funeral throng, a pall,
   A coffin and a shroud.

Three months!—the beautiful, the bright
   Were gathered to her side,
With snowy garlands, fresh and gay,
   To crown the youthful Bride.

To-day they come—no laughing voice
   Each welcomed footstep cheers,—
They come with garlands, pure and sweet,
   All wet with funeral tears.

Alas! how changed,—the Man of God
   Is here, and by his side,
The brave young Bridegroom, trembling, pale,—
   Death claims the blooming Bride.

Ah, Love and Death, strange words—he weeps,
   All desolate and lone—

The Dove, scarce folded to his heart,
 Hath upward gazed, and—flown.

The sunlight of his marriage joy
 Hath set, how soon, in cloud,—
The bridal veil, a winding sheet,—
 The bridal dress, a shroud.

And we, a parted household band,
 We mourn the vanished light,
Whose presence at our fireside shone,
 A sunbeam, glad and bright.

One kiss,—draw near, ye weeping group,—
 Oh, Parents!—sad the hour,
Which from your darkened dwelling, bears
 This beautiful, pale flower.

They come, they come, with garlands white,—
 Ah, wreathe them round her head.
With Orange-flowers and Lily-bells,
 Crown ye, the sainted Dead!

TO ONE IN HEAVEN.

A MOTHER'S LAMENT.

INSCRIBED TO MRS. JOHN O. L. GOGGIN, OF LYNCHBURG.

Oh thou, so early gone!
  Lent for awhile, not given;
Thou who wert here on earth so dear,
  Say, shall we meet in Heaven?

I know that thou art there,—
  Bright, beautiful, and blest;
Shall I, through paths of trial, reach
  The same eternal rest?

Child of my love! I feel
  Thy presence hov'ring nigh,
In every whispering tone that's heard
  In earth, or air, or sky.

26*

The sun with splendor shines
　At morning's dewy hour;
Thy vanished smile I see the while,
　In every opening flower.

The stars look calmly down
　When evening shadows glide,
And then, ah then thou'rt near again,
　An angel, by my side.

Thy favorite haunts I love,—
　In every spot I trace
Some tone or sign, that calls to mind
　Thy dear, departed face.

Ah, whither art thou gone,
　What distant, heavenly sphere
Contains that spirit, glorified,
　So fondly cherished here.

I bow me in the dust,
　I weep when none are near,—

Say, dost thou, from thy starry home,
　　Behold each burning tear?

And art thou less mine own
　　Because with me 'tis night,—
While thou, among the ransomed throng,
　　Art walking in the Light?

Look up! my heart, receive
　　This rod in wisdom given,—
"Endure the cross, and win the crown:"
　　We'll meet again in Heaven.

Child of my love! I seem
　　To see thee even now,—
Harp in thy hand, a crown of Light
　　Upon thy sinless brow.

And thou wilt know me there
　　(What joy the thought hath given)—
Thou'lt know me when through Death's
　　dark vale
　　I go to thee in Heaven.

IMOGEN TO FREDERICK.

WITH A BOUQUET OF PRESSED FLOWERS.

FROM AN UNFINISHED POEM.

" 'He forbids me to write,' said the wife, musingly, 'but I will
send him these pale sweet flowers: they cannot offend; they will
say all that my heart prompts of my unchanging love—of our child
now in Heaven—of the Past—of God. Surely the appeal cannot be
in vain;' and Imogen folded the faded bouquet in a neat envelope,
and enclosed with it a few simple lines."—*Story of "Imogen," by
An Old Schoolmate.*

FLOWERS have a language of mute appeal,
Let these then into thy presence steal;
And let them kindly, though mutely, tell
Of a wounded heart which hath loved you well;—
A heart which unkindness hath bowed to earth,
Whose songs are wailings, whose joy hath dearth;
Oh, let them whisper in soft, low tone,
Of a yearning love which was all thine own;

A love which the tempest and storm have tried,
Clinging 'mid all to thine alien side.
Ah! let them tell of the banished Past,
With its record of fond hopes, flown too fast;—
With its vision fair which, through tears, I trace,
Of a little shroud and a baby face.
Oh! let them point thee to Him above,
Whose arm is almighty, whose name is Love;—
To Him who alone hath the power to save
Earth's sorrowing children beyond the grave:
With all thy burden of errors done,
Still, still look up to that sinless One.

    *   *   *   *   *   *

This be the message I send to-day,
On a perfumed breath from my heart away.—
In all thy moments of mirth and joy,
When sorrows cloud, and when cares annoy;—
In all thy lonely and musing hours,
Hark, to the voice of my faded flowers.

WHERE IS HELEN?

WHERE is Helen?—I have listened long
For the joyous tones of her welcome song;—
I've waited her footstep on the stair;
I've been to her home, but she is not there.

Childhood's sweet voice hath greeted my ear,
With its silvery music, wild and clear;
And daintiest lips, too, my own have pressed
With the fervor of Innocence, pure and blest.

But I look in vain for an eye that shone
With Affection's light as it met my own;
And a form is missed that was wont to glide
With an Angel's gentleness near my side.

I've questioned the flowers if they would tell
Where this bud of my heart may chance to dwell;
But the flowers reply, " We are sleeping low
In our wintry prisons, and may not know."

Then I asked the birds which she used to love,
Whither had wandered the household Dove;
And they warbled an answer wild and clear,
But its mournful melody pained my ear.

I gazed on the clouds as they floated by,
Through the azure depths of the distant sky,
And methought of a radiant clime above,
Where all is gladness, and peace, and love.

Where "little ones" find an eternal rest
In the Saviour's gentle and loving breast;
And Faith whispered low, to my listening ear—
"Earth's brightest and best find a haven here.

"The form thou hast missed lies asleep with the
    flowers;
Thy Bird sings its song amid heavenly bowers;
The crown of the ransomed is on her brow—
The child whom thou seek'st is an Angel now."

MY LITTLE NAMESAKE.

I HAVE a little namesake,
A pet of two years old,
Whose baby features all were cast
In Beauty's fairest mould.

She's a joyous little creature,
As blithe as any bird ;
And sweeter prattle all day long,
I'm sure I never heard.

She tries to play " the lady,"
And takes her little chair,
And places it beside my own
With such a roguish air ;

And with her sweet hands folded,
Her bright eyes fixed on me,

She laughs, to have me notice
　　Her mimic dignity.

But while I pause to praise her,
　　She's up and tottling round;
And such a busy "lady"
　　Can nowhere now be found.

Sometimes she hides, to have me
　　Look for her anxiously,
And if I fail to find her,
　　She'll call out, "*yer is me.*"

And when I walk at morning,
　　I scarcely reach the gate,
Ere I hear her sweet voice calling,
　　" *Oh, Aunty, pese'um 'ait.*"

Then over field and meadow,
　　And up the green hillside,
This little sunbeam follows,
　　An Angel at my side.

She loves the bright-eyed blossoms,
   And not a blade of grass
Can hide its tiny head t' escape
   Her notice as we pass.

The bird, with plumage gay and bright,
   The bee, the butterfly,
All, all are welcomed as they float
   Before her wondering eye.

God bless my little namesake!
   Watch o'er her from the skies,
Until in Death some Angel, bright,
   Shall close her beaming eyes.

THE FEAR OF BLINDNESS.

WRITTEN DURING A PERIOD OF GREAT SUFFERING FROM
ASTHENOPIA.

A BROODING shadow clouds my heart,
   A shadow dark and deep,
Which crowns with gloom my waking hours,
   And haunts me when I sleep.

The strange, wild fear that veiled to me
   Must be Earth's glorious things,
Shut from my gaze each beauteous flower
   Which from her bosom springs.

I dearly love yon arching sky,
   In sunshine and in storm;
Its calm, bright smile, its lightning glance,
   Its rainbow's circling form.

I love the pale, sweet, quiet moon
    That lights that sky at even;
And, more than all, the holy stars
    That gem the brow of Heaven.

I love, ah! well, the woods and streams,
    Mid summer's fervid ray;
To watch the foaming torrent's leap,
    The brooklet's sparkling play.

I love the mountains, old and grand,
    The valleys, green and fair;
The flowers that deck the verdant hills,
    The birds that swim the air.

I love the Sea, the murmuring Sea,
    When calm its blue waves rest,
E'en as a sleeping child might lay
    Upon its mother's breast.

I love it when its billows wild
    In madness darkly roll,

27*

And angry waves swell high beneath
  The storm-king's fierce control.

I love all bright and glorious things,
  The earth, the sky, the sea;
And yet the while I gaze on aught,
  This strange fear haunteth me.

Why is it that the brightest sun
  Thus mocks my yearning sight?
I once could view each dazzling beam
  With rapture and delight.

Why is it from the noodtide glare
  I sadly turn away?—
Alas! to my poor heart there comes
  A pang with every ray.

Yes, strange, dark lines, of late, appear
  Before my burning eyes;
And when I test their waning power,
  Distorted visions rise.

In mercy, Father, close them not ;
    Take not, take not I pray,
That priceless boon which Thou hast given,—
    The boon of sight, away.

Let me yet look in thankfulness
    On Nature's glorious face,
And in her smile or frown the while,
    Thyself, her Maker, trace.

Heal, oh ! my God ; in pity, heal
    These aching orbs of mine,
That e'en on earth I still may see
    Thine image faintly shine.

Ah, let me welcome, as of yore,
    The Day's returning light,
And I will bless the hand which gave
    This priceless boon of sight.

Or if, in wisdom, Thou wouldst not
    Thy threatening rod displace,
Let me, Thy name still praising, still
    In darkness see Thy face.

A DAUGHTER'S PRAYER.

From this low couch of pain whereon he lies,
Whom Thou hast given me, my father dear,
I lift mine eyes, and with full heart, Oh, God!
I pray that Thou wilt hear me from the skies.
'Tis not for us in blindness to arraign
That wisdom which afflicts, or seek to know
The hidden ways, by which Thou lead'st us here
Through paths of trial oft, disease, and pain.
I know that we have sinned and gone astray
From Thy commandments; yet we are, Oh, God!
Thy children still,—as such, then lead us back
To Thee again, through Christ, the Living Way.
Thy chastening hand lies heavily and sore
On one I dearly love;—a father's form
Is slowly wasting from a sure disease,—

Be Thou his strength, Oh. Christ! I ask no more.
Thou who hast suffering known. whose sinless brow
Once drooped in anguish 'neath its thorny crown,—
Oh! from Thy throne in Heaven look kindly down
On him, for whom these tears are falling now.
Lo! through the partings of his thin gray hair,
And on his cheek, a shadowy paleness lies,—
My heart grows heavy as mine eyes behold it,—
I pray Thee. Saviour, make him all Thy care.
Say to disease, away, and let the glow
Of health once more illume his pallid face,—
Bid the weak knees be strong, and once again
Let the cool breath of healing fan his brow.
Give him but length of years, and deign to bless
The filial prayer, adding to this that boon,
"*A hoary head with its bright Glory-crown,*
Found only in the way of righteousness."
Hear me, oh, God! our times are in Thy hands,
The number of our days recorded there,—
Thy voice alone didst say when should begin,
And Thine alone canst stay Life's flowing sands.
Or if it be Thy will that I must see

These dear eyes close in Death's ne'er-waking
    sleep,
In that dark hour open Heaven's "pearly gates"
To him, and send Thy Comforter to me.

"THY WILL BE DONE."

THE twilight deepens into night,
And stars look down with pensive light
    As oft before,
And from yon distant sky so clear,
The gentle moonbeams wander near,
    E'en to my door.

Spring's early flowers,—the Violet blue,
The Cowslip and the Crocus, too,
    Have come again,
And from its moonlit bed of green,
The sweet *Forget-me-not* is seen,—
    Ah! not in vain.

For to my heart the twilight dim,
And night-time with its holy hymn
    Of voices low,

Brings but one picture,—that I trace
In star and flower,—a father's face
    Hid from me now.

My God, I prayed that Thou wouldst stay
The blow, and take him not away
    And leave me here,
For well I knew the world would be
Alas, how dark and drear to me,
    Without him near.

But on that cheerless winter night
When floating shadows dimmed the light
    From hearthstone cast,
I watched a change, though slight its trace,
Pass o'er his patient, suffering face—
    It was the last.

And then they told me he must die,
But resignation's calm reply
    I could not speak.

For love is selfish, and Thy rod
Seemed very hard to bear, my God,
    For I was weak.

And when all motionless he lay,
A soulless shrine of slumbering clay,
    My brain grew wild,—
I said I could not live and see
Him dead, and know that I must be
    An orphan child.

Ah, Jesus,—this poor weary heart
Hath learned to bear, of grief, its part,
    And still throb on.
The broken heart Thou bindest up,
And Thou hast portioned out my cup,—
    "Thy will be done."

Close to Thy cross, oh, Christ! I cling,
Under the shadow of Thy wing,
    Hide me, ah! hide.

Low at Thy feet my spirit lies,—
Look on me with Thy pitying eyes,
    Thou Crucified!

The way is dark, but Thou wilt be
My guide; and clouds and shadows flee
    At Thy command.
Oh! 'mid the waves that darkly roll,
And threaten to o'erwhelm my soul,
    Stretch forth Thy hand.

And though through all Life's sorrowing vale,
My heart sends forth its tearful wail,—
    "Alone, alone!"
Let Thy dear Cross but strengthen me
Always, and all my song shall be,
    "Thy will be done."

A NATIONAL HYMN FOR THE NEW YEAR.

Air—"*Old Hundred.*"

God of the Year!—whose watchful eye
    O'er all Thy great Creation bends;
Whose mercies all Thy children share;
    Whose love to all Thy works extends—
In this our Country's hour of need,
    A Nation's heart bows down to Thee;
In mercy rule the impending storm
    Fast gathering o'er our liberty.

Righteous and wondrous are Thy ways,
    And all Thy judgments true and just—
Ah! let not vaunting Discord trail
    Our glorious Banner in the dust;

That banner, o'er whose stainless folds
  Hath flowed the life-blood of the brave;
For which, in times of danger past,
  Their *all* our fathers nobly gave.

Shall gaunt Disunion hovering nigh
  To our bright flag destruction bring,
While, 'mid the brooding shadows dark,
  Our Eagle droops his wounded wing?
No! show Thy face, Almighty God,
  While peril stalks on every hand;
Stretch forth thine own all-powerful arm,
  And save our own, our Native Land.

Ah, save the Land which gave us birth;
  The Land for which our fathers bled;
Through whose worn paths our infant feet
  Were, earliest, to Thy Temples led.
God! save the Land, in whose blest soil
  Sleeps Freedom's best and noblest son,
Nor let Discord her triumphs boast
  Above the Grave of Washington.

Stay, stay the raging billows, Lord,—
   E'en waves obey Thy great command.
Thou holdest Nations, great and small,
   Within the hollow of Thy hand.
Oh! in this fearful, trying hour,
   Our refuge and our safety be,
As 'mid the tempest, threat'ning, dark,
   A Nation's heart looks up to Thee.

Hide not Thy face in anger now,
   Though we have erred and strayed from Thee,
And in our boasted might, perchance,
   To other idols bowed the knee.
Remember not our wanderings, Lord,
   As on Destruction's brink we stand;
But kindly call, in Mercy's voice,
   And lead us back by Mercy's hand.

God of the Year! receive our prayer,
   In this our Country's trying hour;
Unveil Thy face—stretch forth Thine arm—
   And save us by Thy mighty power.

So shall our praise be of Thy name,
.Our glad hosannas all of Thee,
As o'er Columbia still shall wave
The banner of the brave and free.

January 1st, 1861.